Your friend,
Natalie Popper

Your friend, Natalie Popper

Nancy Smiler Levinson

LODESTAR BOOKS
Dutton   New York

No character in this book is intended to represent any actual person; all the incidents of the story are entirely fictional in nature.

Library of Congress Cataloging-in-Publication Data

Levinson, Nancy Smiler.
   Your friend, Natalie Popper/by Nancy Smiler Levinson. — 1st ed.
     p. cm.
   Summary: In the summer of 1946 Natalie looks forward to going to camp for the first time and being together with her friend Corinne, but things do not turn out as she anticipates.
   ISBN 0-525-67307-5
   [1. Camps—Fiction.   2. Friendship—Fiction.]   I. Title.
PZ7.L5794Yo   1991
[Fic]—dc20   90-40232
                                                CIP
                                                AC

Published in the United States by Lodestar Books,
an affiliate of Dutton Children's Books,
a division of Penguin Books USA Inc.

Published simultaneously in Canada
by McClelland & Stewart, Toronto

Editor: Virginia Buckley   Designer: Richard Granald, LMD
Printed in the U.S.A.   First Edition   10 9 8 7 6 5 4 3 2 1

This book is dedicated to my grown-up cabin mates,
JOANNE, JUDY, CHERYL, STEPHANIE, JILL, and HERMA.

Your friend,
Natalie Popper

1

Natalie Popper followed her friend, Corinne, across the campground. Corinne walked quickly and purposefully with her duffel bag in tow. She had been here at Two Tall Pines for a week the summer before, and she knew all the ins and outs.

Natalie, with her duffel bag and snug-fitting sailor cap from Woolworth's, which Corinne had recommended, marveled at all she saw—the graceful pine trees, the shimmering blue lake, the logs circled around the camp fire spot, the dining building that Corinne informed her was called the mess hall. Natalie felt truly fortunate that she had a friend like Corinne to show her the ropes her first time away from home.

"Corinne?" she called.

Corinne slowed her pace and turned to answer.

"Let's be like glue," Natalie said. "Let's stick together every single minute, okay?"

"Of course we will," Corinne told her, looking astonished

that Natalie felt she had to remind her of such a thing. "Isn't it wonderful? It's just like I described, don't you think?"

"Oh Corinne," Natalie breathed, "I adore it with a purple passion."

Natalie's and Corinne's parents strolled behind them, along with Natalie's little sister, Roberta. The parents were reminiscing and asking one another where the years had gone. Mrs. Friedlander, Corinne's mother, recalled a holiday skit the girls had put together at the synagogue Sunday school back in the third grade, and Mrs. Popper mentioned the blizzard that winter when the girls got lost by the creek and thankfully were rescued by Howie Mann, may he rest in peace. The fathers discussed how eager the girls were to help in the war effort, packing a school record number of Red Cross kits with soap and washcloths and sewing items to send to the fighting soldiers overseas.

"It seems as if it all happened only yesterday," Mr. Friedlander murmured.

Mr. Popper smiled wistfully. "And now look at our little ones. Campers this summer and junior high school students in the fall. Overnight they've blossomed into charming young women."

"Dad-dy!" Natalie said. "Not so loud. People will hear."

She pulled Corinne away and moaned, "I could absolutely die when he does that."

"It's *exasperating*, isn't it?" Corinne said, using an upper-class English accent. Natalie recognized that as a line Corinne had recited from a reading at the McPherson School of Elocution and Dramatic Arts downtown. Corinne had recently started taking lessons there after school on

2

Mondays. That was the day that Natalie helped Miss Hedquist at the library and Corinne rehearsed her lines out loud while Natalie walked her part way to the streetcar stop.

Natalie and Corinne reached the flagpole, where they had been instructed to go, and where the family good-byes would be taking place. They plopped their duffel bags down on the ground, end to end, and sat on them.

"Well, I guess the moment has arrived," Mrs. Popper said with a slight tremor in her throat.

"What moment is that, Helen?" Mr. Popper asked.

"The moment to say good-bye," Mrs. Popper said, starting to choke up. She took a handkerchief from her handbag and gently blew her nose.

Mr. Popper looked at her sternly. "Helen? Remember? We agreed we were going to remain cheerful?"

"I know. I'm sorry. I just can't help it," Mrs. Popper said.

Mrs. Friedlander patted her back comfortingly. "You'll get used to it in no time," she promised. She was already seasoned at saying good-bye to her children, since Corinne attended camp last summer and Corinne's brother, Benjy, had taken a train alone from the Minneapolis depot all the way to Winnipeg, Canada.

Mrs. Popper composed herself and asked where Roberta was. "Has she wandered again? I wish she would stop wandering."

"I'm right here," Roberta said.

Mrs. Popper looked down at her side. "Oh."

"Is it time to go yet?" Roberta asked.

3

"Almost," Mrs. Popper answered.

Roberta poked Natalie and singsonged, "I get the whole back seat on the way home."

"Oh, you are so infantile," Natalie responded with an English accent of her own as she yanked Roberta's hair ribbon.

All around, girls in various colored pleated shorts were gathering, and their parents were issuing last-minute instructions and eliciting promises to behave and to write.

Natalie had already promised to behave and to write home. Now Mrs. Popper told her she had a few other things to say that she wanted Natalie to seriously regard. Natalie sighed and crossed her arms in front of her chest.

"I know you're a good swimmer, Natalie," her mother warned, "but no one is so good that they can go in the water directly after eating."

"I know that," Natalie said in a hushed voice.

"I know you know it, but I also know that sometimes you forget to wait an hour," insisted Mrs. Popper.

"And you don't have to stay in the water so long that your lips turn blue," Mr. Popper chimed in.

Out of the corner of her eye Natalie saw some of the other parents leaving. Mr. and Mrs. Friedlander had waved and were already moving on. Natalie wished she came from a family that issued fewer instructions to their children.

"There's also the matter of health and safety rules," Mrs. Popper continued. "I don't expect you to have any accidents, but if you feel yourself coming down with something you should go right to the registered nurse in the infirmary. And if you hear of anyone else having any symptoms, don't go near them. With all those polio cases in the last few summers, who knows how and where a crippling disease like that will strike next!"

"And one other thing," Mr. Popper added. "The evenings can get very chilly up here in the woods. I don't think it would hurt for you to wear one of those undershirts your mother packed."

"Dad-dy!" Natalie cried. How could he! One camper standing nearby turned and stared at her. The girl was one of the prettiest there, with long, silky white-blonde hair and bangs that came all the way down to her eyebrows. If the camp held an election, she would probably be voted queen of the lake. Natalie was sure the girl had heard everything her parents had been saying. She felt herself turn warm with embarrassment.

Suddenly it was time for the final good-bye hugs. The Popper family was trying bravely to smile. Natalie stood up and busily adjusted her sailor cap and tugged at her bobby sox, one after the other, several times.

"Good-bye and have a wonderful time," Mrs. Popper said as cheerfully as she could, glancing over at Mr. Popper.

Mr. Popper nodded approvingly and then said to Natalie, "That goes double for me, honey."

"Bye, Natalie," Roberta said.

"Bye, Roberta."

Slowly the Poppers turned to leave and started across the field toward their car. Natalie had not anticipated tears, and when they came they took her by surprise. But she blinked them back hurriedly, preparing to explain, in the event that someone should comment, that her eyes were extra sensitive

5

to sun. To be thought of as a baby the first day could mean being considered one throughout the entire camp session. She remembered in first grade how Evie Wissmiller wet her pants in the cloakroom and how people called her sissy and other bathroom names until the day she moved away several years later. From time to time, Natalie had wondered if that was the reason the Wissmillers had moved.

Now as Natalie's family slowly disappeared into the background, a woman stepped in front of Natalie and the other campers and called out enthusiastically, "Welcome to Two Tall Pines!"

"That's the camp director, Midge Sands," Corinne whispered to Natalie. "She's real nice. And that boy with the boots is her son, Dexter. He has a horse."

With the flag waving gently in the breeze, Midge led everyone in the recitation of the Pledge of Allegiance. Natalie thought of Howie Mann, who, like many brave soldiers, had not made it back from the foxholes in Europe. She also thought of Tommy Haverstock, who had sat next to her on the bleachers at the 1946 sixth-grade graduation in the school gym only a week ago. His brother had made it back from the Pacific, but he was wounded and was still confined in a hospital. In deep and abiding reverence, Natalie bowed her head.

After that, Midge quickly livened up the proceedings by calling out, "And now how about a rousing rendition of 'Boom Boom, Ain't It Great To Be Crazy'?" Corinne and many of the other girls knew the words, but Natalie had never heard that song before. She stood silently with her arms dangling at her sides and her mouth closed.

When she looked up she caught the last sight of her family in the distance. They were just driving off in the Desoto. As she listened to the happy voices blend around her, she wondered if her family were driving directly home or if they were going to stop for a black cow ice cream float without her.

～ 2 ～

"That's the head counselor," Corinne informed Natalie. "She's going to call roll and give out the cabin assignments."

Natalie crossed her fingers over her heart as she listened to the names. Finally she heard her own.

"Natalie Sue Popper?"

"Here," she answered, raising her hand.

"Cabin B."

Natalie leaned into Corinne. "Oh, I hope we're together," she breathed.

"Of course we will be," said Corinne with assurance. "We signed up together, didn't we?"

"Corinne Friedlander?" the head counselor called.

"Here."

The counselor glanced at her list. "Cabin A," she said.

Natalie felt a thud inside her chest, and she turned to Corinne and clutched her. "That's a mistake," she said, swallowing hard. "Tell them, Corinne. Tell them they made a mistake."

Corinne put her arm around Natalie and patted her shoulder. "Don't worry," she said. "I'll explain it all to Midge. I told you that she's real nice. She'll work it out right away."

Natalie was glad all over again that Corinne was so knowledgeable about this camping experience. Corinne got up and went right over to Midge, as she promised. While Natalie sat waiting for Corinne to straighten everything out, she turned to the girl who was sitting next to her. Natalie recognized her perfume, one that all the girls were wearing that year. Blue Waltz. She seemed approachable, so Natalie commented on how much she liked the fragrance.

"Thanks a lot," the girl acknowledged, smiling. She introduced herself as Diane Dugin and then introduced another girl as her twin sister, Karen. She was also wearing Blue Waltz. "I think we're in the same cabin as you," Karen said to Natalie.

Natalie regarded the two carefully. Diane had a round pumpkin face with two prominent dimples and rolls of babyfat; Karen was lithe and graceful and had skin far more fair in coloring than Diane. "You don't look anything alike," Natalie said, puzzled.

"Oh, that," Karen said. "We're not identical. We're fraternal."

"Fraternal twins don't have to look alike at all," Diane explained.

"It must really be fun to have a twin," Natalie remarked. The idea of it seemed both wonderful and strange to her. In the past, whenever she had imagined having a twin sister of her own, she had imagined the other girl as an identical mirror image. That, of course, would have been the strange part.

9

"It really *is* fun," Karen said with an impish grin. "We love it, don't we?"

Diane nodded.

By the time that Corinne returned from talking to Midge, Natalie was already feeling much better. "Is everything straightened out now?" she asked, just to make sure.

"Well, not exactly," Corinne answered. "But it will be tomorrow."

Natalie blinked. "What do you mean, tomorrow, Corinne?"

"Listen, don't worry," Corinne told her. "It's just that Midge said it would be too confusing to start making switches right now. She asked if we would please be good, patient kids and sleep in the assigned places for tonight. She promised to work out all the switches first thing in the morning."

Natalie tugged at her bobby sox again, hard. "Oh, but, Corinne, I . . . what . . . what if . . .," she sputtered, unable even to think clearly at hearing this unexpected news.

"I guess there isn't anything else we can do." Corinne shrugged. "Maybe one little night won't be so bad. Really. You'll see."

That was easy for Corinne to say. Corinne knew where everything was, and she knew everything that you were supposed to do. Natalie glanced around at one strange face after another. Her skin felt cold and prickly all over.

The roll call came to an end, and the campers started gathering into their cabin groups. Diane and Karen Dugin waited for Natalie, but she hung back, hesitating to make a move without Corinne.

"Come on," Diane urged.

10

"Who are they?" Corinne whispered to Natalie, glancing at Diane and Karen.

Natalie introduced Corinne to the girls she had just met.

"Oh, now see?" Corinne said, trying to comfort Natalie. "You know two whole people already, so you won't be completely alone."

Natalie was definitely thankful for that, although the fact that those two whole people were twins meant that they probably would be glued to each other every single minute and not want to pay much attention to her.

"Will I be able to see you before the switch tomorrow?" Natalie asked anxiously.

"Natch," Corinne answered, stepping back and looking for the cabin A group. "I'll see you later on. We'll probably see each other a lot of times. Okay?"

Just then a tanned girl wearing an I.D. ankle bracelet came bouncing over toward Natalie, Diane, Karen, and some other girls who were clustered about them.

"Hi! I'm Babs, your cabin B counselor," she announced, flicking her tangled blonde hair out of her eyes.

Babs. That was Natalie's favorite name. It was the one she used when she imagined herself a teenager. A lovely, shapely Babs like this one, not her lanky self with her long "string bean" legs, as her mother called them. And with hair like this one that would whip about her face gently in an open convertible, instead of Natalie's curly hair that grew out instead of down. Natalie truly admired this real Babs.

"Did you all bid your fond adieus to your moms and dads?" Babs asked.

Fond adieus. How wonderfully she spoke too, Natalie marveled. She hoped that Corinne would be moving over to

11

her cabin, and not vice versa, so Natalie would be able to keep Babs as her counselor. Natalie was sure that Corinne would want to have her too.

"Come on. Follow me, ducklings," Babs said, leading her group up a stony path toward the cabin grounds. They had gone only a few steps when someone came running to catch up. It was the pretty girl who had overheard every embarrassing thing Natalie's parents had told her. No doubt she thought Natalie must be a real baby. When Natalie realized she was joining them, she blushed. Now she considered that it might be better if she were moved over to Corinne's cabin. Or the best solution of all—if it worked out that Corinne and this camp queen would be switched. All of a sudden there were so many new possibilities of things that could happen.

Natalie thought of Mrs. Ellenbogen's graduation speech, which had been titled "Taking Flight." Their sixth-grade teacher had told the graduates that they would no longer be in the protective nest of elementary school, but they would be spreading their wings and flying upward and onward. Natalie had looked at Two Tall Pines as marking a truly important occasion of the spreading of her wings. But now it was becoming clear that this camping experience might turn out to be a little more complicated than she had anticipated.

~ 3 ~

Inside the cabin there were eight cots, a row of knotty-pine dressers, and a shredded, small braided rug in the center of the floor. Babs gathered the girls into a circle, cross-legged, on the rug. There was one shy girl, standing alone, biting the nail on one of her little fingers, and Babs gently coaxed her into the circle and placed her next to Natalie. Natalie knew about that nail-biting problem, having only recently conquered it herself with the help of clear polish.

"Okay," Babs began, "we're going to have an icebreaker now. We did this in my college dorm, and it was a real good way to get acquainted. Here's how it works. First you turn to the girl at your right and exchange names. Then you reveal a secret in your life to her. Got it?"

"Any kind of secret?" someone giggled.

"It's a free country," Babs answered. "But the better a cross-your-heart secret it is, the more profound you'll make the friendship." She pointed to the queen. "You're *it*. You start."

The queen's name was Arlette Dahl. It wasn't enough that she was already pretty and had long, silky white-blonde hair. She also had a small beauty mark on one cheekbone to announce her beauty to the world.

Arlette cupped her hands around Diane Dugin's ear and quickly whispered something. Natalie was curious to know what kind of a secret someone like Arlette had.

Diane, of course, sat next to Karen, but Natalie thought that was somewhat unfair if everyone was making a sincere effort to get acquainted with new girls.

To the right of Karen was Marlys Pederson, a girl with long braids, and to her right was Natalie. Marlys revealed her secret so softly that Natalie had to strain to hear. "I brought a lot of candy bars, but don't let anybody know," she whispered. Candy and gum were not allowed and were to be bought only at the camp canteen once each day.

"Oh, I won't, I promise," Natalie assured Marlys. She considered herself a person to be profoundly trusted.

"I have Oh Henrys, Butterfingers, and Baby Ruths," Marlys added, licking her lips.

Now it was Natalie's turn. The shy girl to Natalie's right was named Gretchen Schirmer. When Natalie heard her give her name, she thought she detected a stutter. If that were true, no wonder she was so shy, Natalie thought. Natalie wanted to tell her something that would be heartening to her, so she took a moment to consider some of the secrets in her life. Even though it had happened long ago, there was the time she had impulsively stolen a comic book from Woolworth's. Then there was the crush she had on Alex Keller, a high school boy who lived down the street, even though he had never spoken one word to her in her life. And, of course,

14

there was the secret about the undershirt. None of them sounded particularly worth sharing.

"I'm sorry, but I'm still thinking," Natalie apologized.

Gretchen shrugged and waited.

"That's okay. Take your time," Babs said.

But Arlette sighed loudly and impatiently, making Natalie's cheeks grow hot. Natalie turned to Gretchen Schirmer and suddenly burst out with the foremost thought on her mind. "I'm homesick already," she whispered, feeling tears forming for the second time since she had arrived.

"S-same here," Gretchen whispered in return. "I w-wish I could g-go home."

Natalie's suspicion about Gretchen was true after all. She did have a stutter. A boy in Natalie's neighborhood stuttered, and Mrs. Popper had told her it was because the boy had been born left-handed and his parents had forced him to use his right hand. Natalie wondered if that had happened with Gretchen Schirmer too. She wanted to say something kind to her, but she didn't know what.

The last girl was Judy Waxmeyer, who giggled so much trying to tell her secret that she quit and gave up. When the icebreaker was completed, Babs popped into the center of the circle and asked if anyone wanted to hear hers.

"Your what?" the girls asked.

"*My* secret, you gooses," Babs said.

Natalie marveled that a college girl would reveal something about herself to them. She was so eager to hear anything about Babs's life that before anyone else had a chance to answer, she cried out, "Oh yes!" The others chimed in. "What is it? Tell us!"

Babs laughed. "Sorrrry, I'm not going to tell you now,"

15

she teased in a singsong voice. "You'll have to wait until the end of the session to find out."

Everyone groaned. "Awwwww. Pleeeeese. Not fair."

Babs laughed teasingly again and put her finger to her lips to hush the noise. "For now, let's all get into our bathing suits and take a free swim before supper." Then, right in front of everyone, Babs began yanking off her polo shirt and pleated shorts. Natalie held her breath. She was not the only one who did either. But it turned out that Babs was not stripping in full view of the entire cabin. She already had on her bathing suit underneath her clothes.

Glancing around, Natalie noticed that Marlys Pederson took a long time getting her bathing suit out of the knotty-pine dresser drawer. It was obvious that she was stalling. So was Judy Waxmeyer. Gretchen Schirmer made no move whatsoever toward changing. Neither did Natalie. But Arlette didn't seem a bit self-conscious. She changed right out in the open, and without having on her suit underneath either. What she *was* wearing underneath, though, was a training bra. It was obvious to Natalie that Arlette wanted everyone else to see that she was big enough to wear one.

Babs dumped her clothes in a heap on her corner cot and gloriously emerged in a black two-piece suit and a pair of rubber nose plugs dangling around her neck. She padded back and forth barefooted, supervising the preparation for several minutes before it occurred to her that some girls were hesitating to undress in public.

At that point Babs stopped, put her hands on her hips, and, standing akimbo, asked, "I would like to know how many of you have been in junior high already?"

"I'm going into eighth grade," Arlette answered. "I skipped kindergarten."

"We're in junior high already too," Diane said, pointing to both Karen and herself.

"We're twelve," Karen added.

"Now I'll explain why some of you are a little shy and some of you aren't," Babs began. "When you've been in junior high, you get used to undressing with other girls in the gym locker rooms. See, that's why Arlette and the Dugin girls are comfortable. Of course the Dugins have been undressing in front of each other for a long time. But I assure the rest of you that by next year you will all be perfectly comfortable too. You may even come to appreciate the wondrous miracles of your growing bodies. Anyway, in the meantime you can just go out back to the latrine and change there if you want."

Natalie felt relieved not only for the privacy but for acquiring this useful knowledge, which she intended to pass along to Corinne. Corinne's brother, Benjy, had told them a good deal about junior high life, but of course he never discussed what went on in locker rooms, especially in the girls', which, natch, he wouldn't know anything about. Along with the other girls yet to appreciate the wondrous miracles of their growing bodies, Natalie went out and changed in the privacy of a latrine stall.

Natalie was eager to run ahead to the lake. But Babs insisted they all go together as a group. She also wanted everyone to choose a swim buddy, so that in addition to having the counselor on duty and a lifeguard, the girls could keep a watchful eye on one another. Shyly, Gretchen Schirmer approached Natalie and asked if she would like to be her buddy. Natalie didn't know what to say. She expected to be buddies with Corinne. Gretchen was standing close to her, waiting patiently the way she had during the icebreaker, except this time she nervously twisted a thick strand of hair at the top of her head. How could Natalie say no without hurting her feelings? She would never forgive herself. "Okay," she finally agreed, forcing a wide grin. She tried to sound extra nice about it because she didn't want Gretchen to know that she was really feeling halfhearted.

"Goody," Gretchen said, clasping her hands. "Th-thank you so much, Nat."

Natalie's grin faded. She couldn't hold it any longer. Now she began wondering if a threesome would be allowed in the buddy system. It wouldn't be quite what Natalie had imagined as a perfect arrangement, but it would be better than being alone with Gretchen and having Corinne be buddies with someone else. As soon as possible she was going to have Corinne ask Babs.

Because the number of girls was uneven, Babs did eeny-meeny-minny-mo and took one of the girls for herself. It turned out to be Marlys Pederson. The Dugins were automatically paired off, and that left Arlette and Judy Waxmeyer. Marlys said that she didn't want an older person as a buddy but someone her own age instead. Natalie would not have minded having this particular older person, but she understood what Marlys meant. It made her think of gym class when someone didn't get chosen by a squad leader and the gym teacher took the left-out girl and said, "Why don't you come with me and help carry the bats and the balls?"

Babs asked her ducklings to follow her again, and she led

18

them back down the stony path, through the underbrush, and onto the shore. Clearwater Lake was as blue as the sky, and the ripples in the water sparkled in the afternoon sun. A long dock extended out into the deep water, and beyond that a small floating dock bobbed gently on the water's surface. Several campers were swimming and splashing about.

"It's so beautiful," Natalie murmured to no one in particular, and she scampered across the dock, dived off the far end, and broke into a crawl. Ah! How wonderful it felt. The water was so cold and clear. It was absolutely the most exhilarating feeling a person could have anywhere on planet earth. She was gliding smoothly, stroking and kicking in a nice rhythm, nearing the floating dock, when a shrill whistle broke her reverie. Someone on shore was frantically waving her back. What could that possibly be all about, she wondered, as she obediently turned and swam back to shore. It was the swim counselor who had whistled to Natalie so she could tell her that she wasn't allowed out to the floating dock just yet.

"You have to pass the Red Cross test first," the swim counselor explained. "There are pollywogs, tadpoles, frogs, and dolphins. Only dolphins can go out to the floating dock."

"Oh," Natalie murmured, lowering her head in embarrassment. "I'm really sorry. I didn't know that." It seemed that there were an awful lot of things that Corinne had neglected to tell her.

"That's okay," the swim counselor told her. "It takes a while for new campers to learn the rules. Testing will begin tomorrow."

"I'll t-take the t-test with you," offered Gretchen, who had appeared from nowhere. Then she started to confess,

"I'm not as good a sw-sw-sw . . ." Gretchen was having trouble getting out the word, and it made Natalie squirm.

"Swimmer," Natalie said automatically. When she realized what she had done, her hand sprang up to cover her mouth, but it was too late to take the word back.

"Oh, I'm sorry, Gretchen. I didn't mean to," she apologized, hoping she wouldn't make things worse by calling more attention to the problem. Natalie knew she would hate it if someone did that to her. She resolved never to put words into Gretchen's mouth again, no matter how hard she would have to bite her tongue.

Natalie also realized that Gretchen was saying she didn't know how to swim. But maybe that was a good thing. If Gretchen were only a pollywog or tadpole confined to the shallow water, how could they keep a watchful eye on each other? It would be the perfect excuse to get out of being buddies with her.

Gretchen shrugged off Natalie's blunder and apology, and told her, "I think you already l-look l-like a dolphin in the w-water."

Gretchen's compliment took Natalie by surprise. After what she had just done to Gretchen she didn't think she deserved it, and she felt uncomfortable. Instead of simply saying "thank you" she rambled on in one breath, "Well, I guess I like swimming a lot. We have a lake near my house, and sometimes I stay in the water so long that I turn color and my mom or dad have to yell at me to come out."

At that moment, Natalie looked up and saw Corinne and the rest of the cabin A group heading toward the lake. It was so good to see Corinne that without thinking she dashed off to greet her. Playfully, Corinne snapped her beach towel at

Natalie's behind, and Natalie laughed and grabbed at it. Suddenly she remembered that she had left Gretchen standing alone, and she thought she at least ought to call out and wave to her. But when she glanced over in that direction, she saw that Gretchen, with slumped shoulders, was already walking away by herself.

Natalie lay still like stone on her cot with eyes wide open, staring into the blackness. It was the darkest night she had ever seen.

She had to go to the bathroom desperately, but she could not bring herself to get up, find her way, and go outside to the latrine by herself. If only Corinne were there to help her make the trip. How could Corinne abandon her like this? How could Natalie be a good, patient kid for one night when that night was turning out to be an endless nightmare?

Natalie pictured her bedroom at home with its wallpaper design of little powder-blue umbrellas and her soft bed and chintz bedspread, and her dressing table with the skirt and fitted glass top, under which she had placed her favorite movie-magazine pictures. And just steps away from that warm, comfortable bedroom, which was directly and conveniently across the hall from the bathroom, slept her mother and father, always alert to answer any call or tend to any need.

She listened carefully to hear if anyone else was stirring, someone she might persuade to accompany her, but she heard nothing except the usual middle-of-the night sounds of people in deep slumber. A moment later someone turned over on a squeaky cot and moaned in her sleep, "I'll do it later, Mom."

Natalie's urgency grew worse. She couldn't hold it a minute longer. She had to be brave and get up and go, she told herself. That's all there was to it. But the idea of trying to be brave just to go to the bathroom made her feel foolish. At last she climbed out of the cot and made her way across the room, her arms flailing in front of her, groping like a blind person.

Then the worst happened. She had waited too long. A tiny trickle slid slowly down the inside of one leg. The humiliation of this engulfed her, and she thought she would have a heart attack right there that very moment. It was pitch dark, and everyone was sound asleep, but nevertheless she couldn't help feeling that every single girl knew.

After bumping into a cot and then the doorway, she ran out and stumbled into the night. Just outside the cabin she stepped on a tiny, sharp stone. It shot a stinging pain through the ball of her foot. Tears welled up in her eyes. Suddenly she heard a rustle, and a furry creature darted across the path in front of her. It startled her so that it set off another trickle down the inside of her other leg. This time she let her tears out in full force, and she wept with breathy sobs and small hiccups all the way to the latrine and onto one of the cold toilet seats inside.

She was still sitting in the stall crying and waiting for the heart attack when she heard the outside door open. Underneath the stall, she saw light from a flashlight skitter across the floor and dance toward her.

"Natalie? Natalie? Is that you?" The voice sounded as comforting as her mother's was when Natalie was a little girl sick in bed upstairs. This voice belonged to Babs.

"Yes," Natalie sniffed. "It's me."

"Are you almost done?" Babs asked.

"Yes." Natalie pulled the flush chain, emerged from the stall, and washed her hands, watching the water swirl around the stained sink and disappear down the drain with a gurgle.

Babs soothingly put her arm around Natalie. "You poor lamb," she crooned. "You should have awakened me."

"I was afraid you'd be mad if I woke you up," Natalie admitted. "I was afraid to wake up anyone."

"I'm here to help you at any time, even if it's in the middle of the night," Babs said. "It's my duty as a counselor."

Natalie continued sniffling.

"And maybe there's something else you should know," Babs said. "I'm not only a dutiful counselor, but I also have a calling. In college I'm studying to be a nurse, and I'm going to become a special kind like Sister Elizabeth Kenny. Do you know who she is?"

"Of course I know who she is," Natalie answered. "Everyone in Minneapolis does. The Sister Kenny Institute for polio victims is there."

"Then you know that she came from Australia with new methods to treat those polio victims so paralysis can be prevented?" Babs asked.

Natalie nodded. "Sure. It's always in the newspapers," she said. "My mom and dad talk about it a lot."

"Even though a lot of doctors in the United States think

her methods are a waste of time, Sister Kenny never gives up, does she?" said Babs, her eyes shining reverently in the glow of the flashlight. "She's what I call a noble human being."

Natalie wiped her nose on the sleeve of her pj's.

"Are you feeling a little better now?" Babs asked.

"A little," Natalie answered truthfully.

"Right now you think your homesickness will never go away," Babs told her knowingly. "But I promise you that it will. It will dissolve into thin air soon, and you'll wonder where it disappeared to."

"Do you really think so?" Natalie wanted desperately to believe what Babs was saying, but she found it extremely hard. And besides, right now she was feeling much too much like a really stupid baby. A few days before she had come to Two Tall Pines, she had inserted a new movie-magazine picture of Shirley Temple under the glass top of her dressing table, and it sharply came to mind now. It was a photo of Shirley as a bride, having recently married a war hero in uniform. She was seventeen years old, which was only six years older than Natalie. And when she was Natalie's age, eleven, she had already earned three million dollars. And probably someone so important as Shirley Temple never knew what it was like to feel as if you were a stupid baby, Natalie thought.

Babs yawned, and that made Natalie yawn too.

"Ready to go back to bed?" Babs asked.

Natalie nodded and followed Babs, who led the way with her flashlight. Outside, they listened to the call of an owl in the distance and smelled the fresh fragrances of the night air. When they returned to the cabin in the stillness, Babs tucked

Natalie into her cot and promised her that by morning everything would look much, much better. As Natalie closed her eyes, she imagined the noble Sister Elizabeth Kenny at the bedside of a polio victim, and there working by her side was Natalie's very own camp counselor, Babs.

❧ 5 ❧

"Boo! Here I am!"

From behind her, Natalie felt a pair of hands clamp over her eyes. When she spun around, she saw Corinne with her duffel bag in tow once again.

"I told you that Midge would straighten everything out today, didn't I?" Corinne grinned.

"Oh Corinne, I'm so glad," Natalie said, giving her a quick little hug. "Who's going over there in your place? Is it someone named Arlette?" Natalie crossed her fingers over her heart.

"I don't think so," Corinne said. "It's Judy somebody-or-other. Why? Who's Arlette?"

"She's a girl who thinks she's *sooo* great," Natalie answered, making a face with crossed eyes and sucked-in cheeks. "Wait until you see her and listen to her brag. You'll know exactly what I mean." All of a sudden Natalie realized that with Judy gone, Corinne would probably take her place and become swim buddies with Arlette. This meant reconsidering her earlier idea of forming a threesome. Instead, now she wondered how she might arrange it so that Arlette and Gretchen would be matched up without letting Gretchen find out how it happened.

"Anyway, what's the activity scheduled for our cabin this morning?" Corinne asked, as they headed inside so Corinne could unpack.

Natalie liked the way Corinne had said the word *our*. It righted everything for her once more. "The first thing we're scheduled for is a visit to the nature tent," she answered eagerly.

"Oh, *that*," Corinne grumbled.

At first, Natalie had thought a nature tent sounded kind of fun, and if not actually fun then at least somewhat interesting. But if Corinne already knew that it wasn't either one, maybe the nature tent wasn't worth looking forward to after all. Natalie sat on the edge of her cot with her hands squeezed between her knees and watched Corinne shove her belongings into an empty drawer.

"What comes after nature?" Corinne asked.

"The Red Cross swim test. And following lunch there's beginning canoeing," Natalie answered. This time she tried not to sound overly excited in case Corinne grumbled about these activities too, although Natalie was eager to become a dolphin as soon as possible and to learn how to canoe. Inside her head she was already writing home: *Dear Mom, Dad, and Roberta, Today we went on an exciting and adventurous canoe trip.* The Popper family was sure to be extremely impressed.

Happily, Corinne's face brightened at the mention of canoeing. Natalie was glad about that.

"I never actually got to do it in the water last year," Corinne admitted. "All I got to do was kneel on the dock and practice with the paddle in the water at my side. That's the way they make you learn the strokes. It's not like rowing at all. It's much harder."

Natalie did not know that. She only hoped that the lessons on the dock wouldn't last too long and that she would be able to sit in a real canoe and paddle in the lake.

Marlys poked her head into the cabin. "Babs says everyone's waiting for you kids," she said.

"Okay, Marlys. We're coming in a sec." Natalie smiled. Corinne slammed the drawer shut with her foot, and they hurried out to join the others. Natalie walked with a jaunty bounce.

Everyone followed the sign nailed to the tree, which directed them to the nature tent at the top of a steep incline called Fat Calf Hill. The story went that if you stayed the entire summer and climbed the hill at least once a day, you would return home with big, muscular leg calves. Natalie thought that a lifetime of daily climbs up Fat Calf Hill wouldn't help give any shape to her string bean legs.

The nature tent was the domain of a lady named Winky. During the school year, Winky was a school teacher, and during the summer she was in charge of nature observation at Two Tall Pines. She held the tent flap open as the girls ducked inside one by one.

Just as Corinne was ducking inside, Arlette started to enter also, and they accidentally bumped heads and laughed. Arlette reached up and touched a large silver barrette in her hair. "Thank goodness, it's still there," she said. "I got it at Saks in Chicago. My auhnt bought it for me."

29

Auhnt! Natalie repeated to herself. Whoever heard of anyone calling an aunt *auhnt*?

When her turn came, Natalie ducked cautiously. Inside the tent she found herself near Karen Dugin and a large snapping turtle in a crate. Just as she leaned over it to peer inside, Karen suddenly shrieked. "Look what's next to the box!" she gulped. "A snake!" Karen put her head on Natalie's shoulder. "I feel faint," she whimpered. Natalie didn't know what to do. She had never seen anyone faint in real life before. All she knew how to do was artificial respiration in the event that someone had been saved from drowning, and *that* she had just practiced on a fake victim at the Y. The only thing to do was to alert Babs.

Like a fireman at the sound of an alarm, Babs rushed into action. Swiftly and adeptly, she grabbed Karen by the waist and whisked her outside for some fresh air. Diane was standing near an insect display called Bug Barn. Immediately she stopped whatever she was doing and went after her twin. Even though she was a twin, Diane failed to show any signs of faintness, Natalie noticed. Then Natalie recalled that they were fraternal and not identical, and that probably accounted for the difference in their reactions.

"Is anyone else offended by snakes?" Winky asked loudly from the center of the tent. "Let's see a show of hands."

Nobody raised a hand, but Arlette volunteered that she thought reptiles of any kind were slimy and disgusting, only that didn't make her go and faint about it. Corinne was standing nearby, and Arlette whispered to her that as long as she had to be here she would concentrate on the plants and dead stuff. Natalie didn't think that Corinne would bother answering, even with a brief comment. But she did. And

she said something long too. She said something about feeling like she was in school instead of at summer camp.
Natalie didn't hear the whole thing. Whatever it was,
though, must have been very amusing, because Arlette
laughed with a tinkle voice. Natalie thought maybe Corinne
didn't know she was being nice to the girl Natalie had
warned her about.

Gretchen, who was holding a small painted box, stooped
down and stared at the snake. The sign said it was a Plains
Garter Snake. Upon closer examination, Natalie noticed that
the snake was not alone in the cage. There were also two tiny
white mice with beady red eyes, wildly scampering back and
forth. If anyone had described the scene to Natalie up until
this moment, she would have imagined herself swooning
away in a dead faint too, or gagging. But she was amazed to
find that she didn't have even the tiniest feeling of a queasy
stomach. It was true that it was all slimy and disgusting, and
if she really thought about it in detail she would gag. But at
the same time she found herself really fascinated.

Gretchen called to Winky. "Why isn't that s-snake eating
one of those m-mice?"

Winky brightened at hearing an expression of curiosity
instead of another shriek. She even suggested that all those
who were genuinely interested should gather around. Natalie
moved in, and so did Marlys. Gretchen smiled at Natalie.

"Take a good look at this snake," Winky said to them.
"Tell me. What do you observe?"

There was a pause. Then Natalie saw. "Oh my gosh, there's
a bulge in its middle," she said.

"I s-see it now," Gretchen cried, pressing her nose against
the glass. "You were so quick, Natalie. W-wasn't she,

Marlys?" Then a second later she moaned, "Oh, no. I th-think I get it."

"What?" Marlys asked. "Get what?"

"There's already a m-mouse in there!" Gretchen said, turning toward Winky to see if she was right. "It's already full!"

"Good for you," Winky said.

"The snake ate the mouse whole?" Natalie asked, amazed at both the information and at the snake's ability to perform such a feat.

"That's right," Winky answered.

"It wasn't *dead*?" Marlys asked, startled, and turned to Natalie to see her reaction. Natalie gulped and made a face.

"Snakes won't eat a dead mouse," Winky explained. "They like to catch them. It'll be a few days before that mouse is broken down and digested. So I'm going to take these little white creatures out and save them for later."

Imagine that! Natalie thought. She was sure that Corinne would find this interesting too. When she turned around to call her over, she saw that Corinne was standing at another display with Arlette. They were daring each other to touch a stuffed bat that was mounted on a piece of wood.

"Corinne!" Natalie reached out and grabbed her by the sleeve. "Come on. You've got to see this!" Corinne resisted and glanced at Arlette with a bored expression. Natalie avoided looking at Arlette and tugged at her friend again. "Come on," she urged.

"Oh, I don't know . . ." Corinne said, hesitating. She hemmed and hawed a few more seconds and at last stepped forward. But Arlette flared her nostrils and said, "How re-pulsive!" As soon as she did, Corinne paused and changed her mind. She told Natalie she had enough nature stuff for today. Maybe for the entire session.

Natalie's stomach had been just fine so far, but now it started acting up, and it had nothing to do with snakes or mice or hairy insects. It had everything to do with unexpectedly being deserted by Corinne. How could Corinne do this? The homesick feeling was not dissolving into thin air, as Babs had promised. It was back again in full force.

Finally Natalie said somberly, "Corinne, I have to talk to you in private."

"Is it vital?" Corinne asked. She used an English accent from her elocution lessons, but it was considerably toned down, which was obviously for Arlette's benefit.

Natalie nodded that it was vital.

"Okay." Corinne shrugged. They ducked under the open flap and went outside. Diane was just coming back in. In the distance Karen was sitting on a rock with her head between her knees. Babs sat at her side.

Natalie pulled Corinne away from the tent to assure absolute privacy. She put her hands on her hips, breathed heavily, and asked, "Do you know who that girl in there is?"

"Sure. She's Arlette."

"Then how *could* you?"

"I don't think she's so bad."

"But Corinne . . ." Natalie protested.

"I don't. I just can't help it," said Corinne. "Anyway, I want her to show me how she pin curls her hair. She must do it in some special way because hers comes out so pretty."

"Well, you haven't seen the worst of her. You really don't know how great she thinks she is," Natalie insisted through clenched teeth.

"She took a train trip all the way to Chicago," Corinne added.

"So what?"

"And she has a pen pal in a foreign country."

"Co-rinne," Natalie moaned.

"Anyway, I'm her swim buddy now since that Judy somebody-or-other used to be," said Corinne.

Natalie set her hands on her waist more firmly. "Who told you that?"

"Arlette did. She said you were with that girl who stutters and that you're already best friends. You're the one who found a new best friend first, Natalie."

"I did not! I didn't do anything. And I wasn't going to stay with her either," Natalie almost shouted. "I was going to fix it as soon as I could so you and I would be together. I thought we were supposed to stick together, Corinne."

"We are, Natalie." Corinne tried to reassure her. "I promised, didn't I? Anyway, the buddy system doesn't mean a thing. All it means is that sometimes the swim counselor blows a whistle and you find your partner and raise hands with her so the camp can see that you haven't drowned."

"Oh." Natalie lowered her eyes. She felt a bit ashamed. After all, she couldn't expect Corinne not to talk to any of the other cabin mates. She only wished it hadn't been this particular one.

She looked up, smiled, and said softly, "Listen, that girl who stutters is named Gretchen. And she can't help it, you know."

"I didn't say anything bad about her," said Corinne. "What's in that box she's carrying around, anyway?"

"I don't know," Natalie said. She wondered if it was

something Gretchen was attached to, the way some people were attached to a teddy bear or a favorite lacy pillowcase like Natalie's, although a painted box seemed an odd thing to be hanging onto.

Corinne stood gazing out over a patch of daisies. "I'm going to pick some flowers now," she said. "Want to come and pick some too?"

Natalie really wanted to see more inside the nature tent, but instead she followed Corinne down Fat Calf Hill.

～ 6 ～

"Here we sit like birds in the wilderness, birds in the wilderness, birds in the wilderness," everyone sang loudly in the mess hall. "Here we sit like birds in the wilderness waiting-for-our-food!"

With her fork and spoon waving rhythmically in the air, Natalie joined in the song with enthusiasm and fellowship—"waiting-for-our-food." She had learned these words in short time, as well as the words to the songs "Boom, Boom" and "Kookaburra sits on the old gum tree / Eating all the gum drops he could see / Stop kookaburra, laugh kookaburra / Leave some there for me." When she was able to blend her voice like this in the mess hall or at a camp fire, she marveled at how it filled her with the feeling of pure joy and belonging.

Today's lunch was chili. The kitchen helpers, wearing white bibbed aprons, shuffled out into the hall and plunked a large serving pot in the center of each table. Amid the clatter,

Natalie ladled a heaping bowlful for herself, wolfed it down without looking up once, and asked for seconds.

"I thought you hate chili," Corinne said to her. She sat next to Natalie on the bench, and on her other side sat Arlette.

"I do hate it," Natalie answered. "But I hiked and swam all morning, and I worked up a *ravenous appetite*." That was an expression Babs had used at dinner the night before.

Babs started a plate of bread slices around the table, along with a package of white oleomargarine.

"Ick," Diane groaned when she saw the package. Inside was a yellow disk, which had to be squished around to color the margarine, but it hadn't been squished enough, so it was all streaky. "I thought we didn't have to use this stuff anymore since the war ended," she said to Babs.

"It's a surplus supply that's still used in institutions like prisons, hospitals, and summer camps," Babs told her.

Natalie didn't mind. She took two slices, smeared them with the surplus spread, and wolfed them down also, along with a full glass of milk.

"Do you have a tapeworm or something?" Marlys asked her.

Natalie put down her empty glass and looked across at Marlys. "What do you mean?"

"People who have a tapeworm living in their intestines can eat all day long and never gain a pound," Marlys said. "If they don't get it out, eventually they waste away."

Karen plugged her ears the instant she heard something about a worm.

Natalie seriously considered what Marlys had said. Maybe there was a reason for her being a bean pole—a perfectly good medical reason. She hated going to the doctor, though.

37

First of all, he was a pediatrician, a baby doctor. And second of all, he examined her practically naked and embarrassed her nearly to death.

"How do you get them out?" Natalie asked.

"Don't ask me," Marlys answered.

Babs had been looking on, amused. "I don't think you have that problem, Natalie," she said. "I wouldn't worry about it if I were you."

The kitchen helpers shuffled in with the dessert tray. Tapioca pudding. Immediately, Karen offered hers to Natalie. "Tapioca has little bubble fish eyes in it," she said. "I can't look at it."

Arlette peered into her tapioca dish and flared her nostrils. "I never noticed that before," she said, and also pushed her dessert over toward Natalie. "Anyway, some of us have to watch our figures. Isn't that right, Cory?"

Cory? Arlette was calling Corinne *Cory?* Nobody had ever called her that as far back as Natalie could remember. It was bad enough that Corinne was setting her bangs with pin curls every night to look like Arlette's. And now this! Natalie's whole lunch started to curdle inside of her. She plunked her spoon on the table next to her empty dish, and all the other tapioca dishes suddenly lined up in front of her.

Luckily, she remembered something she had read in the fish unit in science last year in Mrs. Ellenbogen's class.

"Fish eyes remind me of caviar, a very expensive delicacy that's eaten with champagne," Natalie said knowledgeably. Arlette stretched her neck around Corinne and glared at Natalie, as if she had no idea what Natalie was talking about. Then it came to Natalie that caviar was made of fish *eggs* and not fish *eyes*. She blushed, feeling very stupid, and wished there were some way she could take back what she had just said. Corinne didn't come to her rescue either. Natalie looked down at her spoon and stared at her upside-down image in it.

Only Babs's gentle voice distracted Natalie. Babs said that she was worried about Gretchen because she hadn't showed up for lunch, and she didn't want any of her ducklings to miss a nutritious meal. "Natalie, since you're Gretchen's buddy, would you be an angel and run and find her?"

Natalie went only because Babs had appointed her, and therefore it was important to take responsibility. Besides, she had resigned herself to the matchup with Gretchen, although it made no sense whatsoever because they were not matched in swimming ability. In order to pass the Red Cross test to become a dolphin, Natalie had treaded water for three minutes, done the jellyfish float, and satisfactorily demonstrated the breaststroke, the sidestroke, and the American crawl. Gretchen had passed the dead man's float, but that was all. So she was a pollywog and had to remain in shallow water. When the swim counselor blew the whistle, Natalie swam to shore to clasp high-held hands with Gretchen for a camper count. Corinne had been right. After all that worry, the buddy system didn't mean a thing.

Dutifully, Natalie ran up the stony path to the cabin. There she found Gretchen sitting cross-legged on her cot. Her painted box was open, and all kinds of little file cards were spread around her.

"What in the world are those?" Natalie asked.

Gretchen's eyes brightened. "They're m-my animal facts and features cards," she said proudly. "Wh-when I come across interesting facts and features about animals, I write them on these three-by-five cards and file them by animal in this box. S-someday I'm going to m-make them into an encyclopedia."

"What a great idea!" Natalie said. She had never met anyone her age working on a book, let alone a book for a reference shelf. "Can I see some?"

"Do you really want to?"

"Natch. Or else I wouldn't have asked."

Natalie picked one three-by-five at random. It read: "There was once a St. Bernard in Switzerland who rescued a total of 50 stranded and snowbound people." Another read: "Believe it or not, a tarantula feels soft and furry to the touch."

Natalie found this information very interesting. She picked up one more card. It read: "He was the most wonderful there ever was in the world, and I will never forget him. May he be blessed forever and ever."

"What's this one?" Natalie asked, holding it up for Gretchen to see.

"That's just s-something p-personal I wrote," Gretchen answered. "It's about my dog. He was a wh-white terrier mutt named Cotton, and I had him my entire life. Last w-winter he died of old age."

"That's very sad," Natalie said solemnly. "You must have loved him dearly."

"I did."

Natalie paused reverently for a moment. Then she perked up and said, "I have to tell you something really funny."

"A joke?"

"No. A coincidence. I have a box like this at home."

"You do?"

"It's actually a recipe box I got at Woolworth's," Natalie

said, curling her legs up under her as she sat down at the other end of Gretchen's cot. "My cards are on books I read, though. I file them alphabetically by author's last name. Like in the card catalog at the library. On Monday afternoons I help our librarian, and that's how I started this project. I put down the title, author, and a short paragraph about the story. My favorites get a star in the upper right-hand corner."

"That *is* f-funny," Gretchen said. "I mean coincid-dentally. Are any of them animal books?"

The books that Natalie had been reading recently were fairy tales and stories of romance. But she remembered two starred animal favorites from fourth and fifth grades.

"*Lassie* is one, and *Black Beauty* is the other," she answered. "Did you ever read them?"

Gretchen shook her head.

"*Lassie*'s about this beautiful collie who's sold far away because the family is poor, and she tries to find her way home even though a lot of terrible things happen to her on the way." Natalie closed her eyes and shivered just thinking about it. "And *Black Beauty* is about this beautiful black horse who is sold to all kinds of people who treat the poor creature very, very cruelly. Both of them are enough to tear your heartstrings to pieces. They made me cry a lot. You should get them. You'd love reading them and crying too."

Gretchen twisted a strand of hair on top of her head. "Do you w-want to go to the nature tent at free t-time?" she asked.

"Sure. I'll help you with your cards," Natalie offered.

Gretchen's eyes sparkled when she heard Natalie's answer.

Then all of a sudden Natalie remembered the purpose of her coming to get Gretchen, and she slapped her hand over her mouth. "Whoops! I forgot. I'm supposed to bring you

41

back for lunch. Come on. We better go." She didn't want Babs to think she was irresponsible.

Gretchen scooped up her cards, replaced them in the box, and slid the box under her pillow.

On the way down the path, they heard approaching voices singing an Alpine hiking song. Lunch was over, and groups of campers were heading back to their cabins. Babs found Natalie and Gretchen, and took Gretchen aside to give her a stack of bread slices she had wrapped in a napkin for her when she realized that Gretchen wasn't going to make it to lunch in time.

Corinne and Arlette appeared together. Corinne was wearing her polo shirt tucked inside her shorts the way Arlette wore hers. She went over to Natalie and whispered, "As soon as free time starts, we're going to sneak across the road to the corral and see Dexter and his horse. If we act real sweet and sugary he might let us ride. Do you want to come?"

Natalie had just gone and made a promise to Gretchen, and here was Corinne coming up with this. First of all, the idea of sneaking didn't appeal to Natalie. And second of all, neither did going any place with Arlette. It did occur to Natalie, though, that if Arlette knew how to act sweet and sugary in front of boys, she might teach Corinne.

"Well, I promised Gretchen I would . . ." Natalie blurted out, but she stopped herself before going on. If she didn't join them, they would consider her a baby going to a boring baby place.

"G-g-g-gretchen," Arlette mimicked. "How can you stand to be with her? Listening to her drives me bats."

"Natalie feels sorry for her," Corinne said.

42

Maybe Natalie did feel sorry for Gretchen at first, but now she really started to like her.

"Listen," Arlette said to Natalie. "You don't have to come if you don't want to. There's no law about it."

"I know that," Natalie replied. "But I *am* coming with you." She was surprised to hear herself. That was not the only thing that surprised her either. At that moment she turned around and there standing within earshot was Gretchen. She had heard everything. Absolutely everything. Her face looked just the way it did when she had talked about her dearly departed dog. The instant her eyes met Natalie's, Gretchen turned and fled.

Natalie's stomach squeezed in and out, in and out. The taste of chili rose at the back of her throat. She thought of all those people who had so cruelly treated Lassie and Black Beauty, and she felt she was not much better. She felt thoroughly ashamed.

~ 7 ~

"Stroke. Stroke. Stroke," Pam, the canoe instructor, called through a megaphone. "Keep those paddles deep."

Pam and Babs paced back and forth on the dock where the canoers were kneeling along the edge, practicing the basic bow stroke. The girls held the paddles at the grip with one hand and at the top of the blade with the other as they dipped and pulled, dipped and pulled, moving their imaginary canoe swiftly over the swirling rapids.

The canoers were Natalie, outfitted in her sailor cap, Gretchen, Diane and Karen, and a girl from another cabin. Corinne, Arlette, and Marlys had moved onto intermediate canoeing. Natalie thought that she could just as easily have been classified intermediate too, but she was held back in beginning for a very stupid reason—because this was her first time at camp. Her knees were raw and red, but she didn't complain, and she didn't pause for a moment's rest. She worked extra hard so that Babs and Pam would notice how good she was and put her ahead.

"Now let's switch to the J-stroke," the instructor called. "Think of the shape of the letter *J* and you will remember to push that paddle sideways at the end of each stroke. All together now. Begin. Stroke. Stroke. Stroke. Good. Good. Good." Back and forth she paced, back and forth, calling out the paddle strokes like an official coxswain leading the crew of a small boat in competition.

"Oh-oh, Gretchen Schirmer, you're out of synch," Pam called. The megaphone was so close to Gretchen's ear that it startled her and made her drop her paddle into the lake. Immediately it began to float away. Panic-stricken, Gretchen sat and watched it drift. Natalie, who was right behind Gretchen, couldn't let it get away. After that terrible incident on the path she couldn't let another bad thing happen to Gretchen. Acting quickly, Natalie reached her paddle outward at arm's length and caught it. Then slowly she maneuvered it back so that she could easily reach over without falling into the lake and grab onto it for Gretchen.

"It was my fault that Gretchen went out of synch," Natalie said forthrightly to Pam and Babs. "My paddle bumped hers." Natalie didn't consider this a lie. It was more of a fib. But it was a good kind. At home she and her sister, Roberta, were allowed to fib on one condition and one condition only—to avoid hurting someone's feelings. But she had profoundly hurt Gretchen's feelings, and she knew she would never forget it. Not even when she was a very old, forgetful lady would she be able to escape the haunting memory of that incident. For now she was desperate to try to make up for it in any way she could.

When she handed Gretchen's paddle back to her, Gretchen's eyes met hers with a puzzled expression. Even though Natalie had attempted to beg forgiveness several times, they had not actually spoken to each other since the incident had occurred.

Babs squatted down to the level of the canoers and told them to take a rest. "I think they've been practicing a long time, don't you?" she said, looking up at Pam.

Pam sighed and flopped down on the dock, flat on her back, and stuck the megaphone on top of her stomach. "I guess I've been driving them pretty hard," she sighed. "But I think they're ready now."

"Ready? Ready?" the girls cried.

"Do you mean we're ready for a real canoe?"

"Yes, I think so," Pam said.

"Yeah! Hurray! We did it!" Shouts of joy rang out and echoed over Clearwater Lake.

The campers rested on the dock in the afternoon sun for a while. Natalie had been tired from all that practice, but now that she knew she was finally going to get into a canoe like the intermediates, a new energy pulsed through her. A few minutes later, Pam and Babs pulled the two canoes around. Their names were painted on the sides: *Minnehaha* and *Hiawatha*.

Pam spoke briefly and gave some last-minute explanations and instructions. Everyone was required by law to wear a life jacket. Each of the two canoes was equipped with a bailer—actually, an empty coffee can—in case of leaks. Common sense was to be employed by all canoers at all times, and teamwork was of utmost importance.

At last they were ready to get into the canoes. Pam assigned crew positions. In the *Minnehaha* Natalie would be at the bow with Babs at the stern, and Karen and Bunny, from cabin E, as passengers. Bunny complained that she didn't want to be a passenger, but Pam assured her that everyone needed to practice being a passenger and each person would get a chance to practice all positions. Then Karen refused to go in any canoe at all unless Diane was with her.

Maybe it sounded silly to some, but right now Natalie envied such loyalty.

"That's ridiculous," Pam declared in her no-nonsense manner.

"We have to be in the same canoe," Karen begged. "We're twins."

"Oh, piddle," Pam said. "What are you going to do when you grow up? Marry the same man? Anyway, you don't look a bit like twins to me."

"We are!" Karen cried with a tremor in her throat, and she began to shake.

Diane went over to soothe her, and Babs took Pam aside and whispered. Finally Pam said all right, if that was the way it had to be. So she reassigned Karen to the *Hiawatha* as a passenger with Diane, and put Gretchen in her place. When Natalie heard that, she gingerly sidled over to Gretchen and gathered up the courage to tell her she was glad they were in the same canoe.

"Y-y-you didn't have to make up that s-story about your paddle bumping mine," Gretchen said.

"I know, but I wanted to."

"How c-come you did it?"

Natalie's voice dropped very low. "I wanted to help, I guess." She hoped that Gretchen would finally forgive her, but Gretchen said nothing more and took a few steps to the side. This time Natalie decided to make a sacrifice. "Do you

47

want to be at the bow first?" she asked. "I don't mind starting out as passenger."

Gretchen shook her head no and took another step sideways.

The bulky orange life jackets were passed out, and there was some commotion while the campers wriggled into them. When the life jackets were firmly secured, Pam and Babs set about demonstrating proper entry into the canoes. When Natalie got into her position at the bow, she was glad to find that there was a knee pad for her to use.

With a shove from her paddle against the edge of the dock, Babs pushed the *Minnehaha* off.

"Yo-Ho!" Pam cried out from the *Hiawatha.*

"Yo-Ho! Yo-Ho!"

At first it was a little slow and tipsy. But soon the canoers were moving along, at least at a respectable beginner's speed. Natalie dipped and pulled, dipped and pulled, and the glide began to feel a bit more steady. She marveled at how it worked, and at how the early Indians had come up with the idea of making a dugout log to move them swiftly and safely across dangerous waters. Canoeing was hard work, but it was exhilarating. It was more fun than she had imagined. Natalie gazed at the expanse of lake surrounding her as she dipped and pulled in fine teamwork with Babs at the stern. It was just amazing! She was really a canoer now. Yo-Ho!

Natalie felt she could go on canoeing until dusk. Maybe until eternity. But fifteen or twenty minutes later, out of the clear blue sky a gentle spray of rain began to fall. It was a late afternoon sun shower. Natalie wondered if one of the passengers should stand by and be ready with the empty coffee can bailer. She had never thought her first adventure would be so exciting. Surely this was something that Corinne and Arlette and Marlys had never experienced. Wait until she relayed all the details to them.

Before another minute passed, though, Babs and Pam were calling back and forth to each other from the *Minnehaha* to the *Hiawatha*. At first they tried to guess how long the sun shower might last, and when that was not possible, they decided they'd better guide the canoes back to camp. As Babs and Natalie maneuvered the paddles, using sweep strokes to turn the canoe around, Babs explained the reason to her crew.

"We need to hurry back and dry off so we won't get wet and chilled," she said.

Disappointed, Natalie whined, "But we won't get chilled. The sun is out."

Bunny agreed loudly.

Natalie waited for Gretchen to chime in too, but she didn't.

"Well, ordinarily it wouldn't matter," said Babs. "But at last night's counselors' meeting, Midge said polio cases are on the rise, and the Public Health Service Infectious Diseases Department is issuing a list of precautionary measures. One is we're supposed to prevent getting chilled."

Bunny said that was the dumbest thing she'd ever heard. She complained that she hadn't had a chance to paddle yet, and she was going to tell her father to ask for his money back. But Natalie didn't find the situation so dumb. If the Public Health Service of the United States government issued a list of measures of precaution, then that meant serious business. Even though her arms and shoulders ached, she paddled with every last bit of strength to get back as soon as possible.

"Gum chewing is out now, too," Babs added, "since they

think the polio virus enters through the throat, and you know how kids pull gum in and out of their mouths with dirty hands. This was supposed to be announced in the mess hall tonight, but I'm letting you in on this now because of the rain. It's my counselor's duty. And I think it's better to be safe than sorry."

They pulled up to the dock, and the counselors quickly tied up the canoes. Everyone scampered to her cabin. By that time they were wet to the skin, and they were instructed to dry off thoroughly, including having a good hair rub with a towel, and to get warmed inside and out.

Once all the commotion died down, Babs said she thought it would be a good idea for them to have a rest period. This brought loud moans and groans. "You'd think we were in kindergarten," Arlette muttered. When Babs heard that, she said she simply could not remind them enough times that it was better to be safe than sorry. She also told them that the camp was going to institute daily rest periods to prevent their becoming overtired. This, too, was advised, especially for children. Children were particularly vulnerable to coming down with infantile paralysis. That's why it was called *infantile*. The moans grew louder this time. Everyone resented being classified as a child.

Babs announced that she was going to the counselors' tent now, during their rest period, and she expected them all to behave. She snatched up a rain slicker from her drawer and flung it over her head.

"Do they smoke cigarettes in the counselors' tent?" Marlys asked her boldly.

"Absolutely not," Babs hastened to answer firmly, and

somewhat angrily too. "That is *verboten*. What kind of girl would smoke tobacco anyway?"

Natalie certainly couldn't picture Babs or any of the counselors doing anything so icky.

Arlette sucked in a mouthful of air and gasped. "I know. I bet that's your secret you wouldn't tell us before. Is it? Come on. Tell us."

"Absolutely not," Babs repeated. "Anyway, my secret's something good."

"Now I know," Arlette said. "You're really going to sneak off someplace in the woods with a boyfriend. That's what counselors do at night after we're all asleep. That's no secret to anybody."

It was news to Natalie. She wondered how Arlette knew about so many things like that.

Babs laughed. "I told you that you'll have to be patient to find out. For now I want you all *on your cots*! You can talk quietly, but that's all. I'll be back before you know it." And off she went.

Natalie was nervously thinking about this polio situation when hardly a minute later Arlette asked, "Is she gone?" She meant Babs. Before anyone realized it, Arlette snatched up a pillow. *Swack!* She tossed it smack into Corinne's face. Corinne laughed, tossed it back, and then grabbed the pillow from her cot and threw it too. That one missed Arlette and landed on Marlys's head. "Hey!" Marlys yelled. She grabbed her pillow, and still holding it tightly at one end, began whacking against Corinne. All of them were laughing uproariously.

Clearly, Natalie thought, this was not playing it very safe, in view of the polio danger around them and the importance of the precautionary measures. But the laughter grew louder, and Diane and Karen joined in. *Thwack! Whack!* Someone's flying pillow caught Natalie in the face. She had no idea where it came from, but she picked it up and flung it straight at Arlette, catching her by surprise. Natalie was also surprised at how good that made her feel. She wished she had a dozen more to fling at her, one after another. She pictured Arlette sitting on a swing over a bucket of ice water at a carnival booth, and she imagined throwing a ball that would hit a bull's-eye and dump Arlette right into the icy bucket.

Someone's pillow burst open, and a flurry of soft white feathers flew into the air and floated gently over everyone, like snowflakes.

Now the whole cabin was involved except Gretchen. Natalie hadn't intended anything, but all of a sudden she found herself with her pillow in her hand, calling, "Come on, Gretchen. Aren't you going to jump in?" She didn't even wait for Gretchen to answer, but good-naturedly threw her pillow with the lacy pillowcase directly at her. More than anything, Natalie hoped that a smile would break through and that Gretchen would pick up the pillow and throw it back.

"Come on, Gretchen, please . . ."

"N-n-noooo I don't w-w-w . . ." She had trouble finishing her sentence.

Natalie had vowed never to finish another of Gretchen's sentences, and she bit the inside of her cheek to keep from doing it now. "Puleeese, Gretchen," she begged instead.

At last Gretchen spoke. "I'm w-waiting to find out if I can get p-picked up," she said.

52

"What do you mean?" Natalie asked. She thought she knew, but it was the last thing she had considered happening. "You're going home?"

"If-f I can."

"Oh, nooo," Natalie said in a deep, hushed tone. How could she ever make it up to Gretchen now?

"But Gretchen, you can't go home," Natalie begged. "You didn't get a turn to canoe yet. And I really want to go to the nature tent with you, and . . ."

At that moment, Corinne eyed Gretchen's painted box at the head of her cot. It had been covered by her pillow, but with the pillow somewhere on the floor, there lay the box in clear view.

"Oh, can I see what's in your box, Gretchen?" Corinne asked.

Gretchen lunged for it. "It's none of your b-business," she cried.

But Corinne had already opened it.

Arlette shoved herself next to Corinne to get a look. Marlys and Diane tried too, calling, "Let me see! Let me see!"

"G-g-ive it to m-m-me!" Gretchen begged. "It's my p-personal business!"

One by one the cards were snatched from the box, passed around, and scattered into the air with the last few remaining feathers. "This one's doggie stuff," someone sneered, "and this one's kitty-cat stuff."

Crying, Gretchen frantically ran back and forth trying to catch and pick up her cards. Natalie helped retrieve some of them and tried to stop the sneers. When she handed several to Gretchen, she saw her twisted, tear-stained face. Natalie felt

53

her own eyes sting. Finally she drew herself up and cried to her cabin mates, "Stop it! You make me sick!" She was shaking all over.

"Oh, honestly, forget it. Come on, Cory," Arlette said to Corinne.

With that, Natalie spun herself toward Corinne. "I never thought in all my life, Corinne Friedlander, that you could be so mean."

"Well, really, Natalie . . ." Corinne began.

"And don't start that phony English elocution stuff either," Natalie warned.

Corinne took a deep breath and spit back, "Well, it takes one to know one!"

"You think you're so great too now, don't you?" Natalie screamed, her eyes smoldering.

At that, Arlette and Corinne burst out laughing and went off by themselves. Everyone else was dumbfounded, glancing first at Arlette and Corinne and then at Natalie and back again. Quietly Natalie picked up the last of Gretchen's cards. Then she found her pillow with the lacy pillowcase and curled up with it on her cot. Her heart pounded furiously as she lay listening to the soft patter of rain on the roof above.

"Mail call!" Babs announced.

Everyone gathered outside the canteen, but Natalie remained off to the side by herself, leaning against a tree. She watched the girls step forward to receive letters or packages. Gretchen received one letter, which Natalie was sure contained the news that would tell her whether or not she'd be picked up to go home. She'd give anything to find out.

Then Natalie found herself wishing that something would happen to her so that she might have a good excuse to go home. Maybe a broken ankle. No, not a broken ankle. That would hurt too much, and it would mean having to wear a cast and hobble around on crutches. Maybe a sprain.

Corinne and Arlette each received one letter, and Arlette got a small package as well. Arlette opened it and immediately let Corinne peek inside. Natalie swallowed hard. She remembered in vivid detail her first day here at Two Tall Pines when she and Corinne had been best friends and had promised to stick together every minute. Now look what had happened since then. And to think that they had once planned to have a double wedding so they could be brides side by side at the altar in matching wedding gowns.

One minute, Natalie was imagining herself a beautiful bride at the altar without Corinne, while Corinne peered at her through the synagogue window, lonely and full of sorrow and regret. But the next minute, Natalie ached with her whole heart to have Corinne back again the way it was before they had come to camp.

Natalie's name was called, and she hurried forward to get her mail. Her mother had written that she hoped Natalie was continuing to have a wonderful time. She said that everyone at home was fine, and it was very hot and humid. She also said that she had run into Natalie's sixth-grade teacher, Mrs. Ellenbogen, in line at the grocery store. Then she asked if Natalie was eating properly, and dressing properly, too, and making lots of nice new friends. Oh, and by the way, she forgot to mention earlier that the family had bought a brand new automatic clothes-washing machine that was a great time and labor saver.

Roberta added a note on the back of the letter. It was in cursive handwriting, which she was just learning.

> *Dear Natalie,*
>
> *How are you? I am fine. Goodbye.*
>
> *From your sister,*
> *Roberta Popper*

Actually Roberta had accidentally written *Pooper* instead of *Popper*, but crossed it out and rewritten it the right way.

Natalie was just putting the letter into her pocket when she looked up and saw one of the counselors rush over to Gretchen.

"There's a long-distance telephone call for you," the counselor told her. "The phone's in Midge's office. They're holding on. They said it's important." Gretchen hurried off to take her call.

One by one, the campers drifted off across the campground. Babs held only a few remaining pieces of mail, but she paused at one in particular. It appeared to puzzle her. "Miss Karen Audrey Fisk . . ." she read slowly from the envelope, and then looked up among the few campers still waiting. Karen Dugin leaped forward to take it, and suddenly something seemed terribly wrong.

"Are you Karen Audrey Fisk?" Babs asked, perplexed. "I thought . . . I thought you . . ." She paused again.

Karen turned red and glanced at Diane. Diane looked around, clearly not knowing what to do. Babs quickly handed out the few remaining letters and then told Karen and Diane that she would like to speak to them a minute. Natalie remained near the tree where she had been earlier, yet close enough to hear everything. She knew she was eavesdropping, but she couldn't help herself.

"Well, what is going on with you two girls?" Babs asked firmly.

"You tell, Diane," Karen stammered.

"No. You tell," Diane answered, elbowing her. "It was your idea."

"Never mind," said Babs. "You're not really twins, are you?"

57

Karen and Diane shook their heads slowly.

"You're not even sisters, are you?"

They shook their heads again. Karen looked especially sad.

"You certainly fooled everyone," said Babs.

"We didn't mean to do anything wrong," Diane apologized. "It just started out as fun, mainly. I think."

"Just fun? Are you sure that's all?" Babs asked.

Karen shook her head again. "Sometimes I wish so hard that I could really be in Diane's family," she confessed, "that I believe it's come true."

"Where's your family?" Babs asked.

"She doesn't have a mom," Diane answered for her. "And her daddy was shot down by the Germans and had to escape, and he's wounded now, and . . ."

"He doesn't like to talk to me or Grandma very much," Karen said.

Affectionately Babs put an arm around each girl. "I can certainly understand," she murmured. "I won't say anything to the others if you don't want me to. You can tell them when you feel you're ready."

Natalie understood too, of course, even though she was still astonished at what she had just overheard. And to think that she had believed them and even envied them and the loyalty that naturally went with being a twin. Since her fight with Corinne, Natalie had been wishing that she and Corinne were twins, too, so they would have to make up.

But now, of course, that was all changed. Imagine pretending to be in another family because you didn't have a mother. And your father home from war probably in a wheelchair and shell-shocked and haunted with nightmares from seeing the

58

ravages of blood and death. Natalie shivered. She was going to be very, very kind to Karen Audrey Fisk.

Natalie lay peacefully on the floating dock in the midday sun. A long, exhilarating swim had been just what she needed to take her mind off all the confused thoughts that were tumbling about inside her. Now the sun warmed and comforted her as the dock swayed ever so gently, back and forth, back and forth like a cradle.

The gentle swaying did not last long, though. A few minutes later, the dock tilted jarringly to one side as two hands gripped the edge and pulled up a panting and dripping wet body. It was Marlys. She was wearing a bathing cap with a strap tightly fastened under her chin.

"Hi," she said.

Natalie smiled. "Hi."

Marlys snapped off the bathing cap, shook out her braids, and sat down, hugging her knees.

Natalie pulled up her knees and sat hugging them too. There was a quiet moment of reverie, and then she said softly, "It's pretty out here, isn't it?"

"You should see it in winter," said Marlys. "It looks like a scene from a Christmas card."

"Oh, do you come here during the winter?" Natalie asked. "I bet it's a real white wonderland."

"My grandfolks on my mother's side live over in St. Cloud," Marlys answered. "We come up every winter, and we always have perfect Christmases. Do you ever go someplace else for Christmas?"

"We don't celebrate Christmas," Natalie said. "We're Jewish."

There was a pause, and then Marlys blinked and asked, "You are?"

"Hm, hum."

There was another pause, a longer one. Natalie was about to resume her sunbathing, but Marlys said, "Oh. You have one of those Jewish Christmases then."

"It's not Christmas," Natalie corrected her. "It's Hanukkah."

"Oh."

Natalie leaned back on her arms and tilted her face up directly to the sun. A few seconds later she felt the dock tip slightly, and when she glanced over she saw Marlys inching away from where she had been sitting.

"You must be real rich," Marlys said haltingly.

Natalie thought she heard Marlys say something about being rich, but maybe it was something else that sounded like it. "What did you say?" she asked.

"I said you must be rich."

"How come you said that?"

"Because you're Jewish and everything."

Natalie sat up with a start. Marlys was staring at her. Natalie's pulse began beating very fast.

"What are you staring at?" she asked. "And why do you think I'm rich because I'm Jewish? I'm not even half rich."

"I'm not staring," Marlys denied. "And anyway, you know about Jew people having their own banks at home in their attics and thinking they're greater than everybody else. That's why they have big noses to stick up higher in the air. It's true."

Natalie was aghast. "That's the most untrue thing I've ever

60

heard!" she cried through clenched teeth. "You don't even know what you're talking about."

"Well, you don't have to get so mad about it," Marlys said indignantly.

Natalie was trembling inside and out. Those were terrible, unspeakable lies. They were just the kinds of lies told about Jews in Europe that started the Nazis murdering them for no reason and putting them in concentration camp ovens.

"Do you know anything about what happened to Jews all over Europe?" Natalie asked. "Do you? Did you ever see any of those pictures of starving human beings piled up in Hitler's death camps? Tell me that, why don't you. Just go ahead."

"Well, I don't know about those icky pictures," Marlys said, "but if those Jew people over there hadn't gotten so uppity in the first place, then it probably wouldn't ever have happened to them."

Natalie turned away from Marlys. She couldn't look at her another second. She had overheard people say untrue things about Jews before, and she had heard how Jews were called awful names, but no one had ever said them to her like this, face to face. She wanted to shove Marlys off the dock or hit her hard, but she couldn't bring herself to do either. She felt too stunned and hurt to move.

Marlys stood slowly, stretched, and snapped her bathing cap on again. "Oh, listen, I have to go now and see if my ceramic pot in arts and crafts is dry yet," she said, and she dove into the water and swam toward shore.

"There's a tree in the meadow / With a stream drifting by / And carved upon that tree I see / I love you 'til I die."

61

The campers sang in harmony, gently swaying from side to side as they sat cozily around the camp fire.

It was dark outside, and the scattered stars twinkled brightly. The camp fire whooshed and crackled. The faces of the campers shone in its warm glow.

Natalie sat with Karen and Diane. They had told her they weren't twins, and Natalie acted as if she hadn't already found out. She said she understood perfectly. All three girls were wearing Blue Waltz perfume and Diane's mosquito repellent, which her mother said mosquitoes really hated. At Natalie's urging, the three of them together had asked Gretchen to sit with them too, especially after finding out what had happened with Gretchen's long-distance phone call. It had been her parents calling all the way from Fargo, North Dakota. They were there visiting Gretchen's older sister, who had a new baby, and they told her they couldn't come to take her home. Not yet, anyway. But they said they would be there without fail Sunday at visitors' day, and if she was still unhappy by then they would take her right home.

All the while Natalie and Karen and Diane were telling Gretchen how much they wanted her to sit with them, Natalie kept her fingers crossed over her heart. And not in secret either. She placed them right out on top of her sweatshirt so Gretchen could see them. But it didn't do any good. Gretchen had her own heart set on going home. She was just going to wait until Sunday.

Someone threw another big log on the fire, and the flames leapt anew. On the other side of that blazing camp fire sat Corinne and Arlette and a girl from Arlette's school, who sang very loudly and made her voice quiver on high notes. Then there was Marlys. Natalie really, truly hated her. If she believed in voodoo, she would get a doll in Marlys's likeness and stick it with pins and needles on every part of its body so that Marlys would feel the pain everywhere. Through eyes of fury, Natalie watched Marlys offer the other girls a bite of her candy bar. Natalie had never revealed Marlys's icebreaker secret. Natalie always claimed she was a person who could be trusted, and she remained a person who could be trusted, no matter how easy it would be for her to tell on Marlys and get her in trouble. Anyway, next to what Marlys had just said to her that afternoon, hidden candy bars lost any importance they might have had.

Corinne was chomping away on a Milky Way bar, and she smiled contentedly over at Marlys. Natalie wondered if Marlys knew that Corinne was Jewish too. She wished she and Corinne were talking so she could tell Corinne what had happened on the floating dock. She wished even more that Corinne had been there to hear in person, because now she would probably accuse Natalie of making it up, or at least exaggerating what Marlys had said. If Corinne had been there in person, Natalie bet that Corinne would have shoved Marlys overboard in a flash.

In the midst of Natalie's thoughts, someone shouted, "Yay! Here come the marshmallows!"

Midge was scurrying along with an armload of marsh-mallow bags. Dexter carried long twigs that had been whit-tled with a jackknife to a sharp point at the ends. Campers and counselors alike shoved and grabbed until they got their share of marshmallows toasting in the fire. One girl near Natalie said she liked hers burnt black on the outside with a gooey, runny inside, and another girl said, "Ick." Natalie, Karen, and Diane put their marshmallows on one stick and huddled close, all holding on to it together. They agreed to try to toast theirs to an even golden brown on all sides. "Oooh, yum." They also agreed on the good taste.

Soon all the marshmallows were devoured, and the camp fire drew to an end.

Midge led the campers in the evening's final song, "Taps." Natalie linked arms with Karen and Diane and made a point of not looking across the dying fire as she sang.

"Day is done / Gone the sun / From the lakes / From the hills / From the skies. / All is well / safely rest / God is nigh."

❧ 9 ❧

"Race you!" Natalie called.

With her beach towel flying behind her she took off up the path, laughing, and zoomed past Karen, Diane, and Bunny from cabin E.

"Hey, no fair," Karen grumbled. "You got a head start." Karen was quick and light on her feet, though, and as soon as she started running she caught up with Natalie. Diane and Bunny didn't bother joining in the spontaneous race. They stayed back comparing suntans and lifting their shorts to show their suntan lines to each other.

When they reached the cabins, Bunny went into hers, Diane and Karen into theirs, and Natalie headed for the latrine to change out of her bathing suit.

"Meet you at crafts," Natalie called after them. Diane was going to show Natalie how to weave a lanyard whistle chain tightly so it didn't have holes in it. Natalie's first attempt was an ankle bracelet, which turned out awful. At first she was going to throw it away, but she decided she would give it to

Roberta, who wouldn't know the difference, and who would be grateful for a camp memento.

Humming "Boom, Boom, Ain't It Great To Be Crazy," Natalie scampered into the latrine, pattered barefoot into a stall, and tossed her towel and clothes over the top of the door. After that, she peeled off her wet suit, gave it a little shake, and reached for her towel. But the towel had slipped off the top of the door and fallen to the floor on the other side. "Oh darn," she muttered, opening the door and quickly stepping out to pick it up. But as she did, she came face to face with Dexter, who was walking into the latrine with a bucket and mop in hand.

It took only a split second to happen. But it happened. Dexter Sands saw her naked.

Screaming in shock, she leapt back into the stall and slammed the door shut. It was too late, though, and there was no pretending that he hadn't seen. He had been looking right at her, and he saw everything.

"Hey, sorry, kid. Thought it was empty in here," he said, and he left, the mop handle clanking against the side of the bucket.

Natalie could neither move nor speak. Hot, burning tears flooded her eyes, and she stood trembling behind the locked door for a long, long time. Exactly how long, it was difficult to say. Finally Karen and Diane showed up and asked what was going on. When she didn't answer, and she didn't come out, they realized that something was wrong, and they ran to get help. A few minutes later they returned with Babs.

Babs was the only person Natalie would talk to, and even then it took a great deal of patience and soothing reassurance by Babs before Natalie could get the words out. Actually, she never spoke the words directly. By guessing and having Natalie nod in response to her leading questions, Babs figured out what had happened.

"I want to call my mother," Natalie finally said. She no longer cared about being a baby. She just wanted to go home.

"But I'm here," said Babs. "And anyway, I'm sure you'll forget about it in no time."

"I want to go home. Today," Natalie insisted.

"You can't mean that."

"Yes I do, and you can't talk me out of it."

Babs shrugged and shook her head in disbelief. "Well, you are one person I'm really going to miss, Natalie," she said. "I'll miss you on the canoe overnight too. You're cabin B's best man at the bow. I don't know how we'll make the trip without you. Do you still want to call?"

Natalie nodded her head firmly. Her mind was made up.

"Okay." Babs sighed. "Come on then."

"Where are we going?"

"The phone is in Midge's office."

"Midge's office!" Natalie cried. "But what if *he's* there!"

"He won't be."

"How do you know?"

"He's gone into town, that's why," Babs answered. "He drove off in the truck a few minutes ago. He nearly ran me over on the way too."

That sounded convincing enough for Natalie, so she accompanied Babs to Midge's office. Midge was at her desk, with a fan blowing on top while she was engaged in some paperwork. The radio was on, and Frank Sinatra was singing in the background. Babs told Midge that Natalie wanted to make an important phone call because she was very upset about something. Midge asked what that something was, but Babs discreetly answered that it was of a personal nature. Natalie was deeply appreciative of that. She was going to miss Babs, too, and it made her doubly sad about leaving Two Tall Pines.

Midge dialed the long-distance operator and then handed Natalie the receiver to give the operator her number in Minneapolis. At last the call was put through. Roberta answered.

"Roberta? Hi, it's me. Natalie."

"Hi. Guess what? I got a new paper doll set."

Natalie had no patience for anything so stupid right now, and she asked to speak to their mother at once.

"Mommy's not home," Roberta said.

"Is Daddy?"

"Nope. They went out. Mrs. Johnson is here. Do you want to talk to her?"

"No."

"Guess what? Mrs. Johnson burned Mommy's best cooking pot."

"Good-bye, Roberta," Natalie said angrily and hung up. Natalie noticed Babs and Midge exchange knowing glances the way Mr. and Mrs. Popper often did.

"Natalie?" Midge began. "In case you forgot, Sunday is visitors' day. I know your mother and father will be here, and maybe you can straighten things out with them in person."

Natalie could tell that Midge was trying to appeal to her common sense, but this was not a common sense time.

"Thank you, but I'll just sit here and wait to try again, if you don't mind," Natalie said, sitting down on a hard chair and folding her hands in her lap.

"Aren't you coming to the softball game?" Babs asked.

Natalie shook her head.

"We'll miss our shortstop."

Natalie concentrated on her folded hands.

"Okay, suit yourself," Babs singsonged, slowly leaving Midge's office. Natalie knew Babs was expecting her to get up and follow, but she just sat there.

Midge followed, though, and Natalie was left alone with a whirring fan and the voice of Frank Sinatra. Natalie listened to his singing for a few minutes, and she couldn't see why everyone thought he was such a heartthrob.

"N-nat?"

Startled, Natalie looked up. There was Gretchen standing demurely at the doorway.

"I h-eard what h-happened," she said. "I'm really sorrrry."

Natalie's lower lip quivered.

"It must have b-been awful."

"I don't want to talk about it," Natalie said.

Gretchen stepped inside. "Wh-what are you doing here?"

"I'm waiting to call my mother."

"What for?"

"To tell her to come and pick me up."

"You're g-going home?"

"Yes. Today."

Gretchen moved closer. "What about the c-camp out? I thought you could har-hardly wait."

That would be something else Natalie would miss. She was beginning to feel triple and quadruple sad about leaving.

"Well, so what? You're going home on Sunday, aren't you?" Natalie reminded her.

"I guess so."

Natalie paused. "Gretchen, I want to tell you something important," she said softly. "I'm truly sorry about what happened to you too. I never meant anything bad. Really."

"I know it."

After that no one spoke for a moment. Frank Sinatra stopped singing, and a jingle advertising Royal Crown Cola filled the airwaves. Gretchen twisted a strand of hair first one way and then the other. "I'll stay if you do," she said at last.

Natalie shuffled her feet on the floor beneath her chair and then raised her eyes toward Gretchen. "Well . . ." she began, inching toward the edge of the chair. She might as well stay, she thought. "I guess I will."

"Oh, good!" Gretchen cried. "I'm so glad."

Natalie smiled. "Me too."

On the way out, Natalie pressed against Gretchen. "Just promise that you'll let me know every time you see *that boy* coming," Natalie said in a hushed tone, "and that you'll never speak his name in my presence."

"You poor, poor thing," said Gretchen sympathetically. She raised her hand in a pledge. "I p-promise."

∾ 10 ∾

Natalie leaned against the log fence near the Two Tall Pines entrance, waiting. Every time she heard the crunch of automobile tires on the gravel road, she thought it was the Popper Desoto, but it always turned out to be another family's automobile. She couldn't imagine what was taking her family so long, unless they had decided to ride together with Mr. and Mrs. Friedlander.

If that was the reason, then it was understandable why they had not yet arrived. Every time Mrs. Friedlander went someplace, the minute she headed for the front door she changed her mind about what she was wearing. And then she changed it again. Corinne was probably going to turn out just like that too. She was changing her clothes about a hundred times a day now.

Thinking about Corinne made Natalie feel knots in her stomach. She knew deep down she wasn't really as upset about clothes changing as she was about something else. She had never written home about her fight with Corinne. It was

71

just too hard to explain in a letter, and even if she could have explained it in person, her parents most likely would never understand. It seemed easier to pretend that everything was the same hunky-dory okay as it had been the day they arrived at camp.

But there was a very important question that gnawed deeper. Did the Friedlanders know? And if they did, had they told *her* family? She wondered what was going to happen when they were all together at the picnic lunch that Mrs. Popper had planned.

In the midst of these thoughts, Gretchen came running over to Natalie. She was waiting for her family, too, and it was only a few minutes before the tires of the Schirmer automobile came crunching along on the gravel road. Excitedly, Gretchen greeted her mother and father before they even had a chance to open the doors completely and step out.

"I'm g-going to stay," she announced to them proudly. "And so is my fr-friend, Natalie." As soon as Gretchen's parents stepped out of the automobile, Gretchen happily pulled Natalie from the fence and brought her face to face with them.

"So you're the Natalie Popper we've been hearing about," Mrs. Schirmer said. She wore a pretty straw hat with a plaid grosgrain ribbon around the brim. "We're awfully pleased to meet you. Gretchen mentions you in nearly every postcard."

"Thank you." Natalie smiled.

Mr. Schirmer was a thin man, balding, and with kind eyes. He shook Natalie's hand vigorously. Natalie regarded both Mr. and Mrs. Schirmer closely. She tried to imagine first one and then the other forcing Gretchen to write with her right hand instead of her left and causing her to stutter as Natalie had speculated the first day, but she couldn't picture either of them doing such a thing. She was relieved to know they were not responsible, but she wished she knew what made Gretchen stutter so that she could think of some way to help her, especially before starting junior high.

Mr. Schirmer brought greetings to Gretchen from her married sister in Fargo, who had just had a new baby boy, and Mrs. Schirmer showed a snapshot of the baby. His eyes were closed against the light, but Natalie said that she could tell he was an adorable baby.

Gretchen asked Natalie if she would like to come along as she showed her parents around, but Natalie thanked them and said she would just as soon wait for her parents, who were expected any minute. No sooner had the Schirmers started across the campground, though, when Natalie thought she saw Mr. Unspeakable driving his mother's pickup truck. Her pulse quickened, and she pulled her sailor cap down over her eyes, leaving just enough room to see her feet run beneath her. "Wait up, Gretchen!" she shouted. "Wait up!"

Along the way, they spotted Diane Dugin and her parents and Karen standing on the lawn near an area where wickets for a lawn croquet game were set up for the parents' enjoyment. Amidst the group was a wheelchair, but the back of it faced Natalie, and it was hard to see who was seated in it. Diane looked up and waved to Gretchen and her family, and they waved back. Diane waved again, this time beckoning them to come over. Natalie and the Schirmers made their way to the group, skirting around the wire wickets. Then Natalie saw that the person in the wheelchair was a man wearing a military uniform, and he was decorated with two medals. There was something else conspicuous about him, too, but

73

Natalie averted her eyes as soon as she realized what it was. He had only one leg. She thought she knew this man's identity, but she hoped it wasn't who she thought it was because she wouldn't know what to say. Then she'd feel even worse than she did now at the sight of a one-legged man in a cut-off uniform leg pinned together at the top.

The introductions went back and forth, along with handshakes and smiles. At last Karen introduced the man in the wheelchair. "This is Natalie, and this is Gretchen," she said shyly with her hands hooked behind her back. Then she glanced down at his gruff-looking, unshaven face and said, "And this is my dad."

Everything that Natalie had overheard when she had eavesdropped that day at mail call came back to her at once, and she was overcome with sympathy for Karen, her father, and her grandma back home. She had never known a family like this, and she tried to imagine what Karen's life would be like, although it was awfully hard to imagine any other life but her own. Except Natalie knew one thing for sure. If Karen or someone like her lived nearby, she would invite that girl over all the time and make her feel she was part of the Popper family. And if that person wanted to pretend she was Natalie's twin, it would be just fine as far as she was concerned.

It was exactly as Karen had told Babs. Her father, Mr. Fisk, didn't talk much. He just gave Natalie one quick nod. Natalie knew she had been right earlier about figuring out that he was a victim of shell shock. A lot of soldiers came back from the terrible experience of war suffering from it, and it made them sit and blankly stare their days away, while their nights were filled with nightmares.

"Hello, it's nice to meet you, Mr. Fisk," Natalie suddenly

said to him, her hands clammy from nervousness. She was surprised that she was able to speak right out to a one-legged man, but she did it. Maybe, she began to think, if she kept talking to him, really talking about something important, he might be drawn out of his shell shock. Even if it lasted only for a minute, at least that could be a good sign. The subject of war probably wasn't a good one, she realized. What subject *could* she discuss? Hurriedly she sifted through a few possibilities, only none seemed appropriate. Then before she knew it, Mr. Fisk grumbled that the sun was annoying him and he asked Mr. Dugin to wheel him out of it and into the shade. It was too late for Natalie to find the right words or offer any of the help she had intended.

From across the field, Natalie heard her name called. She turned and saw her parents briskly striding toward her. Mrs. Popper carried a picnic basket, and Mr. Popper was holding an old blanket from the front closet. At the sight of Natalie their faces brightened, and Natalie rushed to greet them. She was surprised to see her mother with a new cold-wave hair permanent, which made her look so different that Natalie kept staring to make sure it was still her mother.

Natalie also wondered where Roberta was, but she didn't get a chance to find out right away because the Schirmers and Mrs. Dugin extended their hands and began introducing themselves and exchanging pleasantries. Karen was following her father and Mr. Dugin to the shade tree. Natalie watched them, wishing that Karen's father could walk and that Karen had a mother, and that the whole family could go to their grandma's in the north woods for a winter wonderland Christmas—the kind that Marlys had described just before she had told those hateful lies on the floating dock.

75

After chatting for a few minutes, each family wandered off in a different direction. Only then did Mrs. Popper start to explain Roberta's absence. Barely a word was out of her mouth when Mr. Popper jumped in to silence her. "Helen?"

"Oh, for heaven's sake," Mrs. Popper snapped back. "What's the point of pretending everything is fine and cheerful when it isn't exactly the truth? I don't see any point to it. The Friedlanders went to find Corinne, and they'll probably discuss it with her too."

Natalie flinched. Oh no! They knew about the fight, she thought, and they were going to blame it all on her.

"Discuss what?" Natalie asked anxiously.

"We had to leave Roberta with Mrs. Johnson because of the situation in the city," Mrs. Popper said.

"What situation?" Natalie was relieved that there was no discussion about her and Corinne, but she began to feel alarmed about whatever her mother was going to say.

Mr. Popper smacked his forehead, indicating that he was giving up, and he let Mrs. Popper continue.

"Well, the polio outbreak has reached epidemic proportions," Mrs. Popper went on, "and children all over Minneapolis are being kept at home for the rest of the summer, as a precaution. In fact, I called the pediatrician to ask if we should bring you home, Natalie, but he thought that as long as you were in a contained environment, you might as well stay here until further notice."

Puzzled, Natalie glanced from one parent to the other, and Mr. Popper put his arm around her. "It's nothing to worry about, honey, believe me. No one we know has been stricken, and as long as we follow the precautionary measures we don't have to worry about a thing."

76

This was certainly the last news Natalie had expected to hear. And it was not just news either. It was truly worrisome, despite what her father had said, despite no gum chewing and daily rest periods and not getting chilled or handling dirty money.

Only the sight of Mr. and Mrs. Friedlander and Corinne walking toward them stopped her from thinking about this news. Natalie swallowed several times, although her throat didn't seem to clear.

"Well, look at you, Natalie!" Mr. Friedlander cried. "I bet you've grown a full inch."

Natalie smiled faintly to be polite.

"Oh, I think so too, Natalie," Corinne chimed in, and to the grown-ups Corinne added, "She looks darling, doesn't she?"

Natalie was taken aback. Corinne was acting as if everything were hunky-dory between them. Obviously, she hadn't told her family anything either. Corinne stood next to Natalie and smiled broadly at her, just as sweetly and naturally as could be. Mr. and Mrs. Friedlander had no idea how much of their money's worth they were getting out of their daughter's elocution lessons.

Mr. Popper reached out and affectionately pinched Natalie's cheek.

"Oh Dad-dy," Natalie said, pulling away.

Mrs. Friedlander looked around for a minute, and then asked Corinne, "Say, where is this lovely new friend of yours, dear? Arlette? Is that her name? Your dad and I would love to meet her."

"Her mother and her auhnt took her into town," Corinne answered. "They'll be back later."

"Her *auhnt*?" Mrs. Popper repeated, winking at Mr. Popper. "My, oh my . . ."

Corinne went right on, despite the attention Mrs. Popper had drawn to her new pronunciation. "I know you'll just love Arlette too," she crooned. "Oh, and guess what I forgot to tell you. Her father's an inventor."

"Really?" The grown-ups raised their eyebrows.

Natalie didn't raise her eyebrows, but she was very curious to hear about *this.*

"Yes, he invented a device that clips mittens onto coat sleeves so people won't lose their mittens," Corinne explained. "Isn't that clever? He's expecting his first year's *net profit* to be very high."

Mr. and Mrs. Friedlander beamed at Corinne, and a broad smile spread across the faces of both Mr. and Mrs. Popper.

"Ben," Mr. Popper chuckled, "with talk like that maybe someday you'll end up taking your daughter into the business with you."

"I'm afraid she'll take over the whole company and buy me out." Mr. Friedlander laughed.

Natalie scowled. She could see clearly that everyone thought Corinne had become a real sophisticated person. And all they were able to say about Natalie was that she looked taller, and that was the last thing she wanted to happen. They hadn't even noticed that she was wearing her bobby sox differently. They were folded down, at Babs's clever suggestion. Babs had showed Natalie how the leg tapered at the ankle, and how revealing a bit of that taper could give shape to a leg she called a *slender leg*.

Corinne was standing so close to Natalie now that their elbows touched. "We want to show you our cabin and intro-

78

duce you to our counselor," she said to the grown-ups, and turning to Natalie, added, "Don't we?"

"Oh, su-re." Natalie grinned with exaggeration at Corinne. "Then we can eat afterward. I'm *ravenous*, and I just know the picnic will be *extraordinaire*," she said, although no one remarked on *her* new vocabulary.

The Poppers and the Friedlanders traipsed off to the cabin, where they were given a tour inside the one room and shown who slept on which cot. They were just about to leave and go look for Babs, when she met them on the way in.

"Oh Babs!" Natalie cried happily. "We were coming to find you! Everybody, this is my counselor. This is Babs!"

"It's very nice to meet all of you," Babs said, but she spoke softly and listlessly. Suddenly, she didn't seem like her regular self. She wasn't walking with high, bouncy steps, and her eyes were not sparkling. It was certainly puzzling.

"What's wrong, Babs?" Natalie asked.

"Nothing, little chick," Babs sighed. "Don't worry about it. The important thing is that you and Corinne have a lovely day with your families."

Natalie was deeply disappointed. This was not the special and wonderful Babs she had described in her postcards, and now her parents must be wondering what she had been talking about all along. After leaving Babs, Natalie started to explain to them that Babs was usually a lot of fun, and she couldn't understand what was wrong today. When Natalie paused, she heard Corinne trying to explain the same thing to her parents.

"Babs is so darling all the time," Corinne said. "I wonder why she's acting so strange now."

Natalie realized that she felt equally disappointed and that

79

she also felt bad that something was troubling their counselor. Corinne had been unforgivably mean about Gretchen's facts-and-features cards, but perhaps she hadn't turned into a completely mean person all around.

Mr. Popper spread the picnic blanket in a lovely spot not far from Fat Calf Hill, and Mrs. Popper and Mrs. Friedlander put out all the food. There were corn beef sandwiches on pumpernickel, fruit, dill pickles, lemonade in a thermos jug, and cake with coconut frosting. The only thing missing was the mustard. Mrs. Friedlander said she could just picture it on the kitchen countertop where she had accidentally left it when she departed in a rush.

Natalie and Corinne took turns telling stories about camp. Corinne told about the time she and Arlette saw a live mouse, but nobody believed them, and about another time when she saw a live bat, but nobody believed her then either. Natalie showed a blue ribbon that she had won in a swim race and told about their cabin preparation for the canoe camp out scheduled for the next night. They were going to paddle across the lake, pitch two tents, cook dinner over a fire, and go to the bathroom in the bushes. The grown-ups remarked that they expected that to be quite an adventure. Natalie certainly thought so too.

A few minutes later Corinne started to talk about Mr. Unspeakable. Natalie gasped. Did Corinne know about the latrine incident? Was she going to tell? Miraculously she didn't, and Natalie was spared. It turned out that Corinne only mentioned Dexter's name to explain how she had gotten to sit on his horse.

"Did you ride it?" Mr. Friedlander asked.

Corinne admitted that she hadn't. "But I got to sit on it

80

while he counted to twenty and then he said I had to get down from the saddle," she said, mocking Dexter's voice and waving an imaginary lasso above her head.

Everyone laughed. Corinne laughed too. She was starting to be fun again. She even pulled Natalie aside for a minute.

"Did they tell you about kids being locked up at home because of the polio?" she whispered.

Natalie nodded.

"Are you scared?"

"I don't know. Sort of."

"Me too."

Natalie started to say something else to her, but Corinne asked what time it was because she was beginning to wonder when Arlette would be returning from town.

Soon the picnic lunch ended and everyone joined a tour around the campground. Natalie's parents seemed very impressed by the beautiful surroundings and the camp facilities, and Mr. and Mrs. Friedlander acknowledged that they had forgotten how breathtaking the site was. Then they headed toward the mess hall for the concluding activity of visitors' day—a talent show.

Corinne was doing an English drawing room skit with Arlette. Natalie had done that same skit with Corinne at school one day when a blizzard kept everyone indoors during recess. It didn't seem right that someone else, especially Arlette, was going to play Natalie's part. Just thinking about it gave Natalie a sinking feeling. Today she realized that she still really liked Corinne and still wanted to be friends with her. But sadly, Corinne just didn't like *her* anymore.

All Natalie was going to do in the talent show was sing a new camp song with her cabin. The night before when they

81

were practicing Natalie had thought the song was really cute and funny. And they had all laughed hysterically as they scrounged around for goofy-looking things to wear on their heads while they sang. But as she entered the mess hall now she didn't feel like being cute and funny. With all the things that had happened today, her mind was filled with too many serious thoughts. She didn't want to be a spoilsport at the talent show, though. What she decided to do was forget the goofy-looking beany with the dangling pine cones tied to it that she had planned to wear and just go along with the song as best she could.

❧ 11 ❧

It was a perfect evening for an overnight camp out. Everyone was saying so as cabin B, along with Pam, the canoe instructor, and Maxine, a junior counselor, were loading up the canoes for the trip across Clearwater Lake. There was an old mariners' adage about the weather, Pam said, and she stood on the dock and recited it: "Red sky at night / Sailor's delight / Red sky at morning / Sailors take warning."

No matter what the weather was, Natalie was sure this was going to be a thrilling adventure.

A list of crew positions was tacked to a tree:

Minnehaha	*Hiawatha*	*The Midge*
Stern—Babs	Stern—Pam	Stern—Maxine
Bow—Natalie	Bow—Arlette	Bow—Corinne
Passengers—	Passengers—	carrying tents,
Gretchen, Marlys	Karen, Diane	poles, blankets
		ropes, tools

Natalie wished that Marlys weren't in her canoe. As of late, whenever she was required to speak the simplest remark to

Marlys, even something as easy as "please pass the milk," the words stuck in her throat.

Beneath the crew list was another, which assigned duties and responsibilities, including general loading; life jacket check; blankets, mosquito netting, essentials supply check; food and canteens; pitching tents; cookout fire and putting out the fire; morning cleanup. Natalie was assigned to morning cleanup and to being in charge of the Red Cross First Aid kit at all times.

Despite the attempt at organization, there was still confusion and plenty of problems during the loading process. Some of the food had not been packed watertight and had to go back to the kitchen for repacking. Maxine dropped a jackknife in the water under the dock, Pam scolded Marlys for standing around and not doing her part, and one life jacket was missing.

Natalie was standing on shore, gazing across the expanse of lake when Pam asked her where she found the time to daydream.

"I finished my job," Natalie answered, holding up the First Aid kit. "It's all checked out."

"Well, check it through once more," Pam ordered.

Natalie sighed with exasperation, but went through it again, matching each item against the list of items on the inside cover. Iodine, cotton swabs and sterile gauze pads, tape (narrow and wide), small scissors, tweezers, eyewash, snake bite ointment, poison ivy ointment, aspirin, throat lozenges, and Pepto-Bismol. Something *was* missing, she discovered this time—the thermometer. She didn't go to Pam about it. She went to Babs, of course. Babs told her not to worry, though, because she said she had the natural ability to detect if someone had a fever by a mere touch of her hand on the forehead. Natalie hoped that when she got to be Babs's age she would be so sure about her talents.

Finally the loading was done. The missing life jacket was found, and each camper was secured in one. All girls and equipment were accounted for. Babs, Pam, and Maxine conferred. It was time to shove off.

One by one, the campers climbed into their canoes and took their positions. Natalie settled herself at the bow of the *Minnehaha*. Minutes later the fleet was on its way. Gretchen remarked that she was reminded of Columbus's three ships sailing west on the Atlantic Ocean when he discovered America. Natalie liked that comparison. She turned back momentarily, smiled at Gretchen, and then resumed her paddling. It was hard work as always, but still as exhilarating as the first time. Only now there was a true purpose instead of just paddling out and back or circling one way and then the other.

It was a warm, calm evening. The air smelled fresh, with the pungency of the tall, graceful pine trees encircling the lake. Natalie's nose was filled with their goodness. Occasionally there was a shout from one canoe to another, but most of the time the quiet was punctuated only by the rhythmic lap of water beneath them, the cry of the crickets, and, from time to time, a phrase from the lilting song of a mockingbird.

It was not easy staying together all the time or remaining on a straight course. Pam had to keep shouting to remind paddlers of the best method for staying on course—the

J-stroke. Natalie didn't like the J-stroke. It just about killed her shoulders. When Natalie estimated that they were past the middle of the lake, the point of no return, she asked Babs if she could stop and rest a minute. Thankfully Babs allowed her to, although eagle-eye Pam caught sight of this and shouted to her to get off her duff and get back to work.

"Pam reminds me of Captain Hook in *Peter Pan*," Natalie said, turning to Gretchen, and Gretchen nodded vigorously in agreement. Then Natalie noticed that Marlys had a funny look on her face. She wondered if it were motion sickness. Good, Natalie thought. Marlys deserves to be seasick. Ha-ha for her.

They were now far enough past the point of no return so that their destination came into view. There were shouts of "Land ho! Land ho!" It was a momentous occasion.

When the campers reached shore, they pulled up and unloaded the canoes. Then they dragged them several more yards and heaved them upside down for the night so they wouldn't suffer any damage or slip back into the water. When that task was completed, Natalie stood for a moment with her hands on her hips, turning slowly and surveying all around her. They had arrived. This truly was a thrilling adventure.

"When do we eat?" Diane asked. "I'm starving."

"Me too," said Corinne, hanging her tongue and panting with exaggeration.

Everyone, it turned out, was starving. But the tent had to be pitched first, the counselors explained. So those assigned to that task set about their jobs dutifully, lugging the two canvas tents and the long, awkward poles that accompanied them.

Pam checked the immediate territory and then pointed to a spot, which she said looked like a good one for the first tent.

"I don't think that ground is high enough," Babs said. "Besides there's a tree right there and a gully too."

"That's not really a gully," Pam argued. "It just looks like one."

"Well, if it looks like one, then it must be," Babs insisted.

"Oh, piffle, it's just a little slope," Pam said, and she set to work.

There wasn't much for Natalie to do with the First Aid kit, although her eye was on it at all times in case anyone had an accident. So she helped Karen mix the Kool-Aid in the canteens. Behind them they could hear the tent pitchers still arguing. Pam's voice was the loudest.

"Babs is so much nicer than Pam, isn't she?" Natalie said. "Aren't you glad we got her?"

"That's for sure," Karen answered.

Finally the tents were secured, and the twig-gatherers armed with enough twigs to start the camp fire. Then, at last, the wieners went on to roast. There was also Spam from a can, more war surplus food, and chips and beans. Dessert was everyone's favorite—s'mores. They were made with a toasted marshmallow and a square of Hershey's chocolate pressed between two graham cracker squares.

After supper the sky grew dark, and a gentle breeze came up. The campers carefully doused the fire, and wrapped all leftover food so as not to draw any animals or more mosquitoes or other insects besides those already plaguing them.

Shortly afterward, everyone started getting ready to bed down in the tents for the night. The girls' squealing and laughter rang out in the stillness of the night. "Where are the flashlights?" Arlette yelled out. "I put them on this tree stump, and now they're gone. There's a thief among us." Following a careful, organized search, the campers found the flashlights a few yards away, and each tent received two. And the toilet paper. A roll was hung on a branch at the bathroom site near a short trail behind the tents. Karen had already said she was going to hold it in until they got back to Two Tall Pines—she wasn't taking any chances on going anywhere away from the campsite alone in case there was a snake. Babs told her she might injure her kidneys if she held it in too long, and Karen said she didn't care. Babs offered to go with her, and so did Diane, and then Natalie. Natalie would just as soon have someone at her side, anyway, providing whoever it was would turn around while she went to the bathroom. Gretchen and Natalie made a pact.

Then came the sleeping arrangements. Natalie, Gretchen, Karen, Diane, and Pam shared one tent. Natalie watched Corinne dash along to the other tent with Arlette. To think that she would not be sleeping side by side with her once-best friend on an occasion like this made her feel sad. She also wished she could switch Babs and Pam.

Gretchen admitted to Natalie that she was a little bit afraid of Pam.

"Remember Captain Hook," Natalie whispered.

They laughed and felt better.

It was a tight squeeze inside the tent, but it seemed cozier that way. It didn't matter to Natalie anyway because she was yawning so much that she thought she would fall asleep immediately, even though she had never slept outside in a tent before. Pam slept near the flap, which she rolled down and tied up as soon as each girl called out that she was okay. Pam asked Karen to hold a flashlight while she spread the mosquito netting, then crawled under it herself.

"Okay, you can turn off the flashlight now," Pam said, once she was settled in.

"Can't I leave it on for one more minute?" Karen asked.

"No!" Pam snapped.

Natalie formed her hand into a hooked claw and pressed it onto Gretchen's arm. They laughed again.

"What's that noise?" Diane asked a minute later.

"What noise?"

"Listen. That squeaking noise."

"There's nothing. It's your imagination."

"I heard s-something too."

"Ouch."

"Shhh."

"All right, that's enough out of you guys now," Pam said. "We'll tell some ghost stories, and then I expect you to go right to sleep."

The only ghost familiar to Natalie was Casper, the friendly ghost from the comic book.

Diane offered to tell a story that she had heard at a slumber party. "And it's true too," she said.

"Okay," said Pam. "Everyone, quiet now."

"Well," Diane began, "there was this lighthouse on an island, and the lighthouse keeper brought his young bride there. He promised to stay with her always and forever, no matter what happened."

"I don't have enough blanket," someone complained.

"Shhh."

"I'm starting over," Diane announced.

"No, don't. Just go on."

"Okay. Anyway, one stormy night the lighthouse keeper went out in a boat and never returned. The bride cried day and night until one year later, on their first anniversary, all of a sudden she heard footsteps. They came closer and closer, and her heart pounded louder and louder."

"Eeek!"

"Shhh."

"I'm starting over."

"No. Go on."

"Okay. The footsteps came closer and closer. Then suddenly there he stood! The ghost of the dead husband! 'Come with me, my beloved,' he moaned. So she followed him out into the stormy night. And the next morning her body was washed ashore. The people in the village now say that the two ghosts are still living in the lighthouse. The husband kept his promise to stay with the bride forever no matter what happened, and he really did."

"Oooh, that was very eery, Diane," Natalie murmured.

"And it's true too," said Diane.

It was silent for a moment, and everyone listened to everyone else's breathing.

Then Pam said she would tell a story, and that would be the last one. "Brace yourselves," she advised and lowered her voice as she began. "There was a girl's school set far out in the moors, surrounded day and night by a thick, gray mist."

"Where's that?"

"In Scotland, and no more interruptions!"

"Oh."

"And one day a new girl arrived. Her name was Francesca. She was the most beautiful girl anyone had ever seen. Her skin was like alabaster and her eyes like aquamarine marbles. Wherever she went people stared at her, but she wasn't conceited. She was kind and sweet to everyone. There was one unusual thing about her, though. She wore a thin black velvet ribbon around her neck and never took it off. Never."

Natalie felt her hands begin to sweat. She braced herself.

"The school girls started talking about the ribbon," Pam went on. "Finally someone was elected to ask her why she never took it off. Francesca smiled at the question, but she did not answer.

"Well, curiosity grew until the girls could hardly stand it anymore. They had to find out. One evening one of the school girl leaders had an idea, which she whispered to a small group of her friends. The next day a girl told Francesca that she would like to show her something and invited her into her room. Francesca was delighted and followed her. But as soon as she stepped inside, she was grabbed by several girls who had been hiding.

" 'Oh, please,' she cried. 'Let me go. You don't know what you're doing.'

"But they held her tight, and the leader took hold of the black ribbon and yanked it from her neck. Francesca's eyes flickered, and she gave a tiny little twitch, and then all of a sudden—

HER

HEAD

FELL

OFF and rolled across the floor!"

Everyone screamed bloodcurdling screams.

"And now," Pam whispered, "good night and sweet dreams."

Natalie shivered and buried her face in her arms, sure she would never be able to fall asleep the entire night.

～ *12* ～

"Pssssst. It's raining."

"I know."

"I thought it wasn't supposed to rain."

"So did I."

"Me too."

"Turn on a flashlight."

"What are we going to do?"

Suddenly a clap of thunder awoke Pam, and she sat up startled.

"What's happening?" she asked.

"It's raining."

"I thought you said it wasn't supposed to rain."

"That's what the sky said," Pam answered as she snatched a flashlight, opened the tent flap, and stuck her head out into the night. Everyone was wide awake now, waiting to hear what was coming next.

"It's raining," Pam announced.

"Duh! No kidding!" Diane snapped. "We just told you that."

Natalie could tell that Diane was mad and scared at the same time. She knew that because she felt the same way.

"Well, don't worry," Pam said. "The tent is waterproof, and we're nice and safe inside. Think of all the soldiers who slept under a tent exactly like this and how many storms they weathered."

Another clap of thunder rolled, and the rain came down a little harder. Everyone grabbed hold of a nearby body. Then Natalie felt something on the ground. A feeling of wetness. She could see it with a flashlight too.

"I think the rain is coming in," she announced with a gulp.

"Oh Natalie, it's your imagination," Pam replied. "It's dry as can be in here."

Gretchen touched the spot Natalie referred to and her blanket as well. "It *is* wet in here!" she cried frantically.

"Oh, honestly," Pam sighed, stepping between bodies, and kneeling down to find out for herself. "It's wet all right," she finally admitted.

No sooner had she confirmed this bad news than they heard a chorus of terrible shrieks outside. It sounded like all the voices from the other tent. A minute later, Babs came rushing over to them. Then the rest followed, squeezing themselves inside and crawling over one another to take shelter. A branch had fallen on them, and their tent had collapsed.

"I told you to pitch the tent on higher ground and not under a tree!" Babs shouted at Pam. "But *you* know everything. Now look what's happened!"

"It's getting wet in here too," Natalie told Babs.

"Yikes!" Babs threw up her hands. "Any minute now there's going to be a river flowing through here."

"P-U, this wet wool blanket stinks," Karen said.

"So what are we going to do, Pam-who-knows-everything-in-the-world?" Babs asked defiantly.

"Listen, don't blame *me* for everything!" Pam snorted.

Natalie had never seen Babs so mad before. She plugged her ears to try to block out their voices like she did at home sometimes when she heard her parents argue. She just wished Babs would be her regular, comforting self and get them all back to their cabin safe and sound.

At that moment Marlys whimpered loudly. She really irked Natalie.

"What's wrong?" Babs asked Marlys.

"I don't feel good," Marlys answered.

Babs reached out to her immediately. "Here, let me feel your forehead."

Natalie held one of the flashlights and shone it on Babs, watching her press the palm of her hand across Marlys's forehead for several seconds.

"I think you have a fever," Babs announced. This seemed to give her more ammunition for attacking Pam. "This is a terrible predicament we're in," she wailed. "We have this little lamb, and Corinne with a twisted ankle from falling over Maxine . . ."

Corinne was *injured*? Natalie swung her flashlight until the beam of light found her.

95

"You twisted your ankle?" she asked.

"It hurts something awful, too," Corinne moaned.

"I have the First Aid kit," Natalie offered. "I could tape it up."

"Arlette already wrapped her bandanna around it," Corinne told her.

"Oh," Natalie said.

Meanwhile, Babs and Pam's argument had grown nastier, and Babs's voice was trembling. "Well, we certainly can't stay here," she said. "*You* are going to have to run out to that farmhouse, Pam, and ask if we can stay the rest of the night in the barn."

Sleep in a barn with barnyard animals! Natalie didn't know whether that would be icky or fun.

"Why me?" Pam asked.

"Because I can't leave a sick person, that's why," Babs answered angrily. "And we can't send these kids either, you know. You and Maxine will have to go."

"Me too?" There was panic in Maxine's voice.

"Yes, you too," Pam said. "What if something happened to me on the way? Who would get the message back here?"

"It's getting wet under my seat," Arlette announced.

"Obviously, I'm the only one with enough guts to lead the way," Pam said, getting up and tugging at Maxine.

Natalie removed the blanket that she had wrapped around her. "Here," she said, holding it out to Pam. "It's not a rain slicker, but maybe if you and Maxine put it over your heads it might help a little bit."

Pam, who was standing but stooped forward to keep from bumping the top of the tent, took the blanket and shined her flashlight on Natalie's face. "I didn't think of that," she said. "Thanks." Then she and Maxine ducked out and ran for it.

"What if they don't make it?"

"What if the people there are mean and tell them to get off their property?"

"Yah. What if nobody's even home?"

Babs cleared her throat. "I'm not allowing any more negative talk like that. Do you all understand?" she said. "That's not the way to behave in times of emergency. People survive by helping each other, not making things worse." Babs was speaking with calm and surety once again. Natalie felt better.

"Shhh!" Arlette said suddenly. "I hear something."

"I hear it too," Diane said.

"I don't."

"What?" Natalie grabbed Gretchen's hand.

"It's a growl!" Arlette gasped. "Oh no. I bet it's . . . a . . . bear!"

Screams rang out, and Marlys moaned pitifully.

Babs tried to calm the girls, but there was too much panic now for anyone to pay attention. Arlette insisted the bear smelled them and was coming closer and getting ready to pounce.

Suddenly Gretchen sprang up on her knees and announced loudly, "Okay, listen, everyb-body!"

Arlette was so surprised that she stopped shrieking and listened.

"There are no b-bears living in this area," Gretchen said.

"Oh, yah, sure . . ." Arlette muttered.

"And even if they did, they w-would not come and p-pounce on us." Gretchen explained this so clearly and directly that she sounded just like a teacher at the front of the classroom. Natalie sat up proudly next to her.

"I don't believe you," Arlette answered.

"I don't c-care if you do or not," Gretchen said nonchalantly. "Bears are peaceful, and m-most of the time they run away from danger, and they aren't afr-fraid of people. They j-just attack if someone is going to hurt one of their cubs."

"Well . . ." Arlette hesitated.

"These facts are t-true, aren't they, Natalie?"

They were. Natalie had read them in Gretchen's box.

"Yes, they are, Arlette," Natalie said firmly. "So just quit being such a stupe and making things worse for everybody."

Everyone was quiet for a second. Finally Arlette mumbled something, but she spoke so softly she could hardly be heard above the rain.

A minute later they all heard another noise.

"Oh no. N-not again."

"Maybe it's Pam and Maxine."

"I hope so."

"It's not. It's a rumbling."

"It's a truck! It's the pickup!"

"Yay! Hurrah! We're saved!"

It *was* the truck. Natalie gasped—but this was hardly the moment to worry about Dexter Sands or to think of her own embarrassment. It was relief enough that he and Midge had come to their rescue, and that they had also found Pam and Maxine on the way.

Much of the stuff was left at the campsite to be retrieved the next day. But since Natalie had the Red Cross First Aid kit, which she had guarded throughout the adventure, she carried it with her onto the truck. Once everyone was settled, Natalie felt a tap on her shoulder. It was Corinne.

"This dopey bandanna is wet, and it isn't helping a bit," she said. "Would you tape up my ankle now?"

Dutifully, Natalie pulled out the roll of wide tape and carefully began winding it around Corinne's ankle as the pickup truck made its way over the bumpy road, delivering the dripping canoers back to camp.

～ 13 ～

All those who had been on the camp out were required to stay in bed—under covers—for the entire day. Natalie even put on the undershirt she had hidden at the bottom of the drawer. Under the circumstances it seemed a wise thing to do.

Breakfast was brought into the cabin, and the girls were required to eat a full bowl of hot cream of wheat and drink a glass of orange juice fortified with a teaspoon of cod-liver oil. Later the camp nurse came in and began swabbing their throats with iodine. It was a miserable, gaggy ordeal, but nobody protested too loudly because it was understood that it was something that had to be done.

One person from the cabin was missing—Marlys. As soon as the truck had arrived back at Two Tall Pines, she had been taken directly to the infirmary. Now, as the nurse made her way from cot to cot, a strange feeling hung in the air. Finally Babs asked the nurse how Marlys was doing, and she answered that Marlys had a touch of fever and a mild sore throat, but she was coming along fine and would be back romping in no time. The nurse told the girls not to worry their little heads about a thing. There were some whispers and giggles after that, but to Natalie they seemed like the kinds of giggles people had when they were nervous. That was the way Natalie felt, anyway.

In the afternoon, Midge brought her office radio into the cabin to distract the girls, and they listened to a soap opera and then a popular program called "Queen for a Day." Several contestants told really sad stories about their lives to explain why they thought they deserved to be crowned Queen for a Day. The winner, whom the audience chose, was a lady with eleven children whose husband had an accident while he was repairing the roof. Her prizes were a set of Fiesta Ware glazed pottery dishes, a Come-Clean carpet sweeper that sweeps faster and easier, and an imported string of pearls. Natalie glanced at Karen, who was reading a Wonder Woman comic book. Maybe her grandmother could get on that program, Natalie thought. She liked that idea a lot and was eager to share it privately with Karen later.

By early evening everyone was very restless and ill at ease. Corinne fell asleep for a few minutes and awoke with a start. Natalie hugged her pillow tightly. Babs decided it was a good idea to entertain everyone, and she told about a heartthrob war hero named Audie Murphy, who was now starring in the movies. The girls seemed so relieved to be entertained that Natalie offered to tell the plot of a book about a Russian girl who grew up to become a great ballet dancer and danced at the czar's palace. Then Arlette started describing a movie called *A Song to Remember*, which was the true story of a piano composer, Frédéric Chopin. As Arlette related the story, Natalie realized that Arlette wasn't acting stuck-up about it. She was describing the romantic scenes so beautifully that Natalie wanted to see the movie. Arlette was just about to tell the ending when Bunny Miller and Judy Waxmeyer appeared.

"We wanted to see how you were," Bunny asked.

"Yah, we heard you almost drowned," Judy chimed in.

Babs smiled. "That goes to show how rumors circulate," she said. "No, we didn't almost drown. We're all fine."

There was a pause and then Bunny said, "Guess what?"

"What?"

"Something strange is going on around here."

Judy looked out the window and then back at the girls. "There's a big gray car outside. And it's parked on the lawn."

"So?" Karen asked.

But Babs jumped up to take a look. The others, including Natalie, followed.

"I don't get it," Diane said.

Natalie didn't either, but she didn't say anything. She noticed, though, that Babs looked very serious. Then Babs used a serious tone to tell everyone to stay put and she would be right back. But exactly at that moment another counselor appeared, grabbed her aside, and whispered something to her. Whatever she whispered, it left Babs visibly shaken. Babs leaned against the wall and tried to catch her breath.

Everyone clambered around the two counselors, insisting that they tell what was wrong. Finally, explaining that it was her duty to inform the girls, Babs gave in. "There is very bad news about Marlys, and this is not a rumor," she said solemnly. "Marlys has been stricken with polio."

The purple twilight was closing in over all Two Tall Pines camp. Natalie stood outside in the shadows staring through a clearing at the infirmary where Marlys lay. Arrangements had been made for an ambulance to pick her up and take her to the nearest hospital.

Gretchen stood at Natalie's side. "Do you think she's p-paralyzed yet?" Gretchen asked. "What if she has to g-go in an iron lung to do her b-breathing f-for her?"

Natalie shrugged. She didn't know any answers. Nobody did. It was too early to tell how Marlys would end up. Nobody even knew yet exactly how people caught polio.

Suddenly Gretchen grabbed Natalie's arm and looked her straight in the eye. Natalie could see that a truly awful thought had just occurred to her. "Do you th-think . . ." Gretchen began ". . . that Marlys might *die*?"

Natalie shook her head slowly and mechanically. She just stared straight ahead, even though she had no idea what she expected to see happen across the way. Karen and Diane were walking in circles nearby with Babs. They didn't seem to want Babs to leave them. Every time she moved, they followed and asked her another question.

Natalie didn't dare speak out loud to anyone the questions and thoughts that were on her mind, not even Babs. She had never imagined anything as terrible as infantile paralysis, but she *had* wished ill upon Marlys. Now, of course, Natalie felt really sorry for her, except somehow she couldn't get herself to feel as deeply sorry as she would if it were someone she liked.

A breeze came up and sent a slight shiver through her, and she went into the cabin to put on a cardigan. Corinne was lying on her cot with her taped ankle propped up.

103

"Does it still hurt?" Natalie asked.

"I don't know." Corinne shrugged.

"Do you want me to put more tape around it?"

"Uh-uh."

There was a pause.

"It's really scary now, isn't it?" Corinne asked.

Natalie nodded.

"I'm more exposed than you are," said Corinne. "I ate from her candy bars."

Natalie remembered. She looked at Corinne mournfully.

Then Natalie noticed what Corinne was wearing around her neck. "Is that the bandanna you bought at Woolworth's?" she asked.

"Uh-uh."

"I didn't think so."

"It's the one Arlette gave me. She told me to keep it."

"I guess that means you're friends with her forever," Natalie said wistfully.

"But *we're* still friends too, you know," Corinne said. "Aren't we?"

Natalie was surprised. "I thought you didn't like me anymore," she said.

"That's what I thought you thought about me," Corinne admitted. "Are you mad?"

"A little bit," Natalie said truthfully.

At that moment Arlette came in and perched herself on the edge of Corinne's cot. "Hi," she said to both of them.

"Did the ambulance come yet?" Corinne asked her.

"I don't know," Arlette answered. "Midge said it's not going to have the siren on."

"Oh," Natalie and Corinne said together.

Gretchen, who was looking for Natalie, tiptoed in and gingerly closed the screen door behind her. "I th-think it's coming," she whispered.

"The siren's not going to be on," Arlette said.

"I know," Gretchen answered. "But s-someone said they s-saw it."

There was a pause.

"Now what do you think will happen?" Natalie asked.

Nobody said anything.

~ 14 ~

Immediately after breakfast the next morning all campers were requested to gather outside by the flagpole for an announcement. Natalie could see the gray car parked on the lawn again, and this time another car was parked alongside it.

As soon as Midge got everyone's attention, she introduced a man named Dr. Washburn.

"Dr. Washburn is from the Infectious Diseases Department at the U.S. Public Health Service in Washington, D.C.," she said in a choked voice.

Dr. Washburn rolled up his shirtsleeves and loosened his tie and top shirt button. Then he turned to address the campers. Natalie tugged at her sailor cap.

"I'm here—" Dr. Washburn began slowly "—on serious business. You probably all know the news by now that one of your campers here has been diagnosed with infantile paralysis."

Everyone did know, of course, but gasps came from all

106

directions at hearing the words spoken by an authority from Washington, D.C.

"We don't want you to be unduly frightened," Dr. Washburn continued, "but as I explained, dealing with this baffling disease is serious business. So an important decision has been made in regard to your camp." He paced back and forth several steps before announcing what that decision was. "I'm sorry to tell you that Two Tall Pines will be closed down at once," he said with his head lowered. "I am sorry."

Natalie's heart tightened. So much was happening so fast. This was baffling too.

Midge stepped forward again. "All of your families have been notified," she added, still choking, "and you are all requested to go directly to your cabins, pack your belongings, and wait for your transportation home."

One by one, the bewildered campers made their way up the stony path for the last time. Inside cabin B, Marlys's empty cot stood as a grim reminder of the cruel tricks that life could play.

Everyone went about stuffing her belongings into her duffel bag. It was as quiet as the first day when they had all arrived new to one another. Natalie remembered the icebreaker and the get-acquainted secrets, and she reminded Gretchen of how she had whispered her admission of homesickness. Now she would bet anything that when she got home she would be lonesome for camp.

At mention of the icebreaker, the girls suddenly realized that Babs had never revealed her cross-your-heart secret as she had promised she would do at the end of the session.

"Come on, t-tell it now," Gretchen urged.

"No, I don't think this is the right time for something like that," Babs answered.

"Oh, come on."

"Pleeese." Everyone pleaded.

"Oh, all right," Babs sighed, sitting cross-legged on the braided rug. "But I have to explain to you that it's not the same secret that it was. It's turned into a kind of bittersweet story."

Natalie sat down next to Babs and listened eagerly. She wondered if the day that Babs wasn't her regular, happy self had had something to do with the bittersweet event.

"At the icebreaker I was going to tell you that I got pinned by my boyfriend, Wayne," Babs said. "That means getting engaged to get engaged. Anyway, one night when we met in town . . ."

"See," Arlette interrupted, "I told you the counselors have boyfriends they sneak out and meet."

"Shhh."

"Well, that night I realized that I wasn't really in love with Wayne. I was only in love with the *idea* of love," Babs continued. "Things didn't happen perfectly the way I thought they would. Things just changed. I wasn't the same person anymore, and I had to be true to myself and give Wayne back his pin."

That was for sure, Natalie said to herself. When she had arrived at Two Tall Pines she thought everything was going to be perfect for her too. The way it had been comfortable in the protected nest that Mrs. Ellenbogen had talked about at graduation. But things had just changed. With Corinne and Gretchen, and Arlette, and even Babs. The war hadn't happened only in Europe either; it had reached out and hurt people everywhere, including right here at her summer camp in the woods. And now Natalie knew a girl who had fallen victim to infantile paralysis. Natalie still couldn't bring herself to like Marlys, but she sincerely hoped that Marlys Pederson would not be crippled or lie in an iron lung for the rest of her life, or even die.

After Babs finished revealing her bittersweet secret, she snatched her Brownie camera and had everyone pose for a group snapshot. Only minutes later, some of the family automobiles began to arrive. Mr. Dugin came for Diane and Karen, and he waited patiently as the girls went around the room and hugged each person good-bye. It was very tearful. With two people gone, the cabin felt empty.

Arlette's "auhnt" arrived at the same time as the Schirmers, and there were more good-byes. Natalie told Arlette that as soon as the kids in Minneapolis were allowed to leave their homes again, one of the first things she was going to do was see the movie about that piano composer.

Natalie and Gretchen hugged each other tightly.

"Promise to write me tonight," Natalie sniffled. Her eyes filled with tears.

"You have to p-promise too, no m-matter how late it is," said Gretchen. She sniffled louder.

"I will." Natalie wiped her nose and waved as Gretchen disappeared with Mr. and Mrs. Schirmer.

Pam arrived with a message for Natalie and Corinne. "The Popper and Friedlander automobiles are parked at the entrance," she said, "and your families want you two to hurry as fast as you can. Get moving now, you kids! On the double!"

Natalie missed having Gretchen there so they could laugh at their Captain Hook joke.

109

Babs hugged Corinne and wished her lots of good luck. As Corinne said good-bye, she burst into sobs. Then she turned to Natalie and said, "I'll call you up tomorrow morning, okay?" and limped away.

Natalie picked up her duffel bag, and Babs held the door open for her. "You did a beautiful job taping up Corinne's ankle," Babs told her. "I think you have a special touch that's gentle and quite *magnifique*." With a warm and tender embrace Babs wished Natalie all the luck in the world.

"Thank you," Natalie said, smiling through her tears. She would never forget her counselor or anything at camp this summer as long as she lived.

Natalie stepped outside of cabin B and paused as she watched a sparrow alight momentarily on a branch, then spread its wings and take flight again. Good-bye, little bird, Natalie whispered. Good-bye, Two Tall Pines. And with sure, quick steps she set off along the stony path, blinking against the bright morning sun.

Babs Schumacher
100 Spring St.
Red Wing, Minnesota

September 16, 1946

Dear Babs:

I just love the cabin group snapshot you sent. I put it under the glass top of my dressing table. Thanks a ton.

As you can imagine, the rest of the summer staying home because of the polio epidemic was a big bore. I was really glad when school started. The first week at junior high was

*kind of scary. We have different classes and bells ringing
all the time (as you know, natch) and at first I was always
afraid of being late. But I got used to it, and I like it a
lot now.*

*For math I have a man teacher. What a heartthrob! Pant!
Pant! Corinne is in my gym class. Guess what! You were
right about what you told us on the first day. We don't mind
changing in the girls' locker room. You were right about
the tapeworm too. I went to the doctor's for a checkup and
found out I don't have one.*

*I hope you are fine. Did your college start yet? What
classes do you have? Do you like your ~~teachers~~? Oops. I
mean professors? Do you have a new boyfriend yet?*

Lots of love from your friend,
Natalie Popper

About the Author

NANCY SMILER LEVINSON is the popular author of several nonfiction and fiction books for young readers. Her books include *Christopher Columbus: Voyager to the Unknown* and *I Lift My Lamp: Emma Lazarus and the Statue of Liberty,* a 1987 Child Study starred book.

Ms. Levinson lives in Southern California with her husband. They have two sons.